D0436214

WE ARE LOST AND FOUND

WE
ARE
LOST
AND
FOUND

Helene Dunbar

sourcebooks fire

Published by Sourcebooks Fire, an imprint of Sourcebooks
P.O. Box 4410, Naperville, Illinois 60567-4410
(630) 961-3900
sourcebooks.com

Library of Congress Cataloging-in-Publication data is on file with the publisher.

Printed and bound in the United States of America.
LSC 10 9 8 7 6 5 4 3 2 1

For those we lost...
And for those who found their voices.

All through the years of our youth
Neither could have known
Their own thought from the other's,
We were so much at one.
—*William Butler Yeats*

We've got to live,
    no matter how many skies have fallen.
—*D. H. Lawrence*

PART

DECEMBER 1982

On the last day before Christmas break, Mr. Solomon hands out a bunch of sharpened number two pencils and a stack of Xeroxed sheets. Just answer honestly, he instructs our class, It's a career-assessment test, not a final exam.

The first question:

Which tasks would you prefer to undertake (select as many as apply):

→ *Arrange flowers*
→ *Sell products*
→ *Study the cause of diseases*

→ *Make people laugh*
→ *Drive a truck*

I hesitate and write my own list in the margins, drawing boxes and filling them in hard until the pencil tip is ground down to nothing.

→ *Fall in love*
→ *Figure out who the hell I am*
→ *Have sex without catching something*
→ *Repair my family*
→ *Escape*

St. Sebastian's is glowing with candles, swirling with incense, and overrun by kids allowed to stay up way past their bedtimes to attend midnight mass. But the only thing I can focus on is my brother, Connor, drumming his fingers on the wood of the back pew, trying to pretend he doesn't care that he's sitting alone in our family's church on Christmas Eve.

When Dad goes to talk to someone he knows from work, I whisper to my mom and ask if she can find a way to get my father to allow Connor to sit with us.

She looks back at my brother, who is wearing a bizarrely conservative button-down and cardigan. The only part of the getup that looks like Connor is the BEAT IT button over his heart. Even when he tries to rein it in, he can't.

Connor glances over and then looks away. He knows we're watching.

For a minute, I'm optimistic. After all, it's Christmas and Connor didn't have to come to St. Sebastian's. He has a million friends. A world of boys he's replaced us with. He only came to this church because he knew we'd be here. That *has* to count for something. Even to my father.

But then Mom spins her wedding ring and says, It's a holiday, Michael. Let's not make waves. You know how your father is.

And any hope I have for a Christmas miracle is dashed faster than an eight-year-old's belief in Santa Claus.

My parents would murder me if they knew I was standing outside Central Park at midnight on New Year's Eve with my best friends.

They'd murder me twice if they knew I was drunk.

But Becky brought a flask of something that goes down like fire, and it's freaking cold out, so we pass the container back and forth, while horses pull tourists around in carriages behind us. Then, in unison, we tilt our heads toward the sky, watching the clouds move across the moon, while the whole city explodes in noise and light and the possibilities that 1983 might bring.

Time kind of stops, and I hold my breath, trying to hang on to this feeling. We're standing shoulder-to-shoulder—Becky, James, and me—for warmth, or friendship, or safety, or something I can't name. James is in the middle as always, binding our little group together simply by being James.

He's wearing this long, black, wool coat with tiny anchors etched onto the silver buttons that might make anyone walking by think he had military leanings, but the sharp architectural cut of his white-blond hair and the gray slash of his eye shadow would set them straight.

Next to him, I look like a mannequin for Sears's Young Men's department in my sweater and jeans, while Becky is channeling that new singer, Madonna, all teased hair, rubber bracelets, and a fishnet shirt under her blue wool pea coat.

James reaches an arm around each of us.

I lean my head on his shoulder, careful to avoid his TEARDROP EXPLODES: TREASON button.

Becky reaches behind his back and grabs my hand, her skin cold through her black lace gloves.

You know what, Michael? James asks, as he steps forward and turns to face us, backdropped by the fireworks, arms open wide as if he could embrace the entire city.

I shake my head and watch the snowflakes fly off my hair, each perfect crystal reflecting the flash of colored lights: red, green, gold.

Becky moves closer to me, either to wait for the wisdom of James, or to warm up.

This is it, he says, in the quiet space between explosions. The silence is so gigantic, it's as if all of New York reserved this moment to hear what James has to say. And what he says is: This is the day it all begins.

What? Becky asks.

James looks at the sky as if he owns it and says, The best year ever.

And that is how I know I'm drunk—I believe him.

I'm the only one of us stuck with a curfew.

I have to be home by one thirty—a New Year's Eve reprieve

from my usual midnight deadline—because my mother worries.

And because my father is a control freak.

The question is always this: Use the bulk of my allowance to take a taxi—if I can even find one—or risk my life and take the subway?

A slideshow plays in my head. Graffiti-decorated trains and silent cars where no one will meet your eyes and, this time of night, the smell of piss and vomit, and lights that dim when we hit certain parts of the tracks.

Take a taxi, Becky says. Money won't help if you get stabbed.

James grabs her from behind in a bear hug, his head resting on her shoulder. He says, Oh, kitten, that will never happen. Don't forget that Andy and his new friends will swoop in like Spider-Man to protect Michael from the bad guys.

Becky has been dating Andy since the middle of sophomore year. BeckyandAndy, AndyandBecky.

Once Andy found out he only had to be sixteen to join the Guardian Angels, he started training to become a card-carrying vigilante, like he's doing tonight.

James rolls his eyes. Must make the subway safe for the tourists, he says under his breath.

Becky scowls and pulls away. James shrugs and says to me, Or spend the seventy-five cents on a token and buy the new U2 import single. You know you want it.

There *is* that.

Really? Becky asks me with her hands on her hips. Really? You can't wait, like, two weeks for a record to come out in the States?

James and I stare at her with matching expressions.

I love you, Becks, but you don't get it, I say.

And she doesn't get it. She listens to music, follows the fashions, but to her, it's all background noise. Something to cover up the sound of traffic and the neighbors screaming at their kids, and to take her mind off the fact that it's New Year's Eve and her mom probably won't come home or even call.

Music isn't the thing that makes her feel alive.

I try to stand next to the cop on the subway. Try not to stare at the hundred-year-old woman with the accordion, or the girl reclining on the lawn chair, or the guy talking to himself and rattling the door between the cars, or the two kids at the end of the car with gang tats.

I try not to think that maybe Becky was right.

JANUARY 1983

The three of us spend the first day of the new year at a place in Chinatown with no English menu. The fun of it is pointing at the signs on the wall and eating things we can't identify.

When we're too full to move, too talked out to focus, James pays the check, and the waiter brings us fortune cookies.

Becky's fortune says she'll come into money. She laughs as if it's the funniest thing she's ever read and sets the paper on fire by holding it over the candle on the table until the slip turns to ash.

Mine says, Change can hurt, but the pain always leads to something better. I read it twice and shove it in my pocket, pretty sure I'll be awake all night trying to figure out what it really means.

James's cookie is empty.

What the hell? Becky asks. Her hair is in a long braid, and it swings emphatically as she shakes her head at the affront.

James pushes his bangs out of his eyes and gives her a reflective look.

I guess I get to write my own future, he says.

This sums up the difference between me and James. I would have assumed that a cookie with no fortune meant I was going to be hit by a truck.

After, Becky suggests we go to a party. She has a friend who has a friend whose older brother has a houseboat docked at the 79th Street Boat Basin and is celebrating 1983.

Are you sure they won't mind us coming along? I ask.

Oh, Michael, she says looking me up and down, no one will even notice you're there. Besides, they're only making spaghetti. Not like you eat that much.

James hesitates because he knows I hate inviting myself places, hate the feeling that I might be intruding.

He says, I have an idea. Then he leads us into a bodega where he piles a mountain of Ronzoni noodle boxes on the counter and gives the clerk a twenty. He stuffs the change, well over five bucks, into the cardboard charity collection box that's raising money for a little girl with cancer.

The clerk stares at him. At his long, white-blond, New Romantic hair, at his cat-eye eyeliner, at his favorite powder-blue linen jacket—the one with the linebacker shoulder pads, cinched waist, and rhinestone belt.

You ain't up to something, are you? the guy asks.

James doesn't answer, but shakes his head as we walk out. Sometimes you can't win, he murmurs under his breath.

Will Andy be at the party? I ask.

Becky fiddles with her braid, her all-black watch wrapped around her wrist, reflecting the sun.

I don't think so, she says. He's on duty again.

James coughs deliberately, and I knock my shoulder into his.

James thinks Andy isn't good enough for her. But aside from the fact that Andy loves to patrol the creepiest parts of New York City and help make citizen's arrests, he isn't that bad. He brings Becky presents every Friday in homeroom. Flowers from his mother's rooftop garden. Iron-on patches for her favorite ripped jeans. Song lyrics scrawled on rough, old paper.

Becky loves him, she says. She wants to marry him someday, she says.

But then, she says, there are times I wish he weren't so nice. We never fight, so we never get to make up. It's kind of boring.

The houseboat is rocking from the weight of the people (which is a lot) and the weight of the weather (which is threatening to turn ugly) and the expectations of the partygoers (which are as high as they are, considering that the cloud of pot smoke hanging over the deck is thick enough to blot out the moon).

Someone shoves a Bartles & Jaymes wine cooler in my hand but disappears before I can thank them. James appears out of nowhere with an open bottle of Asti. He grabs my drink and sets it on a counter. Then he takes a slug of the bubbly wine before handing me the bottle and gesturing for me to drink.

Before I take a sip, he says, This year you will create music. You will fall in love. You will find your place. You will be happy.

Only James can say things like this without sounding sloppy drunk.

Yeah? I ask, daring him. And how exactly do you know?

He leans in close. I can smell the alcohol mixed with cigarettes on his breath. It's not at all unpleasant. His mouth is up against my ear, his words only for me. This is your year, Michael, he says. Trust me about this.

And the silly thing is, I do.

Last night's snow didn't stick, and now there's a loud Trivial Pursuit drinking game happening up on the roof deck. I'm about to suggest that James join in, because I don't know anyone as good at remembering obscure facts as he is, but then a bunch of guys throw the host overboard.

James winces and says, You can't even fish in the Hudson; everything here is contaminated.

The guy surfaces, sputtering. He's hauled up from the freezing river by the same people who threw him in. They're all drunk and hooting, while he's laughing and dripping water and who-knows-what-else all over the floor.

I watch the guy strip off his wet coat and clothes. The

alcohol and pot have dulled my reflexes, and my gaze lingers on his abs long enough that James has to cough to get my attention.

Do you think he knows about the pollution? I ask.

I doubt he cares; it's the danger of being young, James says, as if he weren't just eighteen himself. You think you're invincible.

The conversation spreads through the party like the wave at a Yankees game.

He's queer, how did I not know…? I mean, he doesn't *look* like a fag… Well, *I* knew… Shut up, you did not… Well, I do now…

Acid rises in my throat. I forget sometimes.

Forget that I'm not transparent.

Forget that if I just stay silent, no one will know this piece of me.

Forget that, unlike James, I can hide in plain sight and let them assume what they want. If I take Becky's hand, they'll think we're together. That I'm one of them.

And that makes me feel sicker.

James twists a ring and takes a drink. It's hard to know where he ends and the actor begins. He's heard this all and worse before, of course, but his face is impassive. Perhaps he's used to it. Perhaps he's able to tune it out. Perhaps he has his own way of hiding.

Later, James and Becky and I stand out on the deck. Prince's "1999" plays inside. I wonder where we'll be in sixteen years. In our thirties, I guess, which is bizarre to even think about.

It's a clear night under a full moon, and we're out here so Becky can do her monthly ritual of trying to emotionally let go of things, although I'm never really sure what she's trying to let go of.

James leans back against the railing, his eyes to the sky, a thoughtful look on his face.

I hover over Becky's shoulder, close enough to be surrounded by a cloud of Love's Baby Soft perfume, and watch as she writes *fear* on a piece of paper towel with a black Sharpie, and folds it into a square.

She holds out her hand, and James wordlessly passes her a slim, silver lighter as if they'd choreographed their movements. Then she lights the paper and throws it over the side of the boat. It hits the water, sizzles, and sinks.

Well, says James in a voice dripping with sarcasm. There you go. I guess we're all safe now.

The next day, I take the rest of my allowance to collect my reward for braving the subway on New Year's Eve.

B-Side Records is my father's worst nightmare. New albums in on Tuesday. Comics on Thursday. A steady stream of rich kids, poor kids, weird kids, gay kids, kids who smell like pot, kids who smell like booze, kids who just smell.

Music is the great equalizer: $7.99 for an LP. $5.99 for a cassette. Twenty-five cents for all the used stuff in the bargain bin.

I could easily spend every dime I have in this store, but I stay focused and head to the import section. UK 45s have this tiny hole in the middle, like an LP, instead of a big hole like

U.S. singles. Thankfully I have an adapter, a yellow piece of plastic with RHINO RECORDS stamped on it to use with the rest of my singles, so I can stack the U.S. and UK ones together on my turntable's spindle.

The import section is decked out with a million flags from a million different countries, even though 90 percent of the records are from the UK. The British flag is red, white, and blue. I don't get why the colonists hated England enough to declare war on them but stole their flag colors anyhow.

I think about James and his British mother. About how there's so much tension between them all the time.

It's funny how sometimes you can speak the same language, yet you still need a piece of round plastic to bridge the gap.

I met Becky and James at a fire drill two weeks into my freshman year. When the bell went off, I followed the other students into the hallway and then through the door as they trudged out to the street on a dreary day.

Everyone knew everyone else. Except for me.

It took a minute to notice James fitting himself into a doorway, marking up a paperback with a highlighter he kept bringing thoughtfully to his lips.

But then I couldn't stop noticing him, couldn't look away from his bright white shirt, sleeves rolled up to the elbows, or his gray striped suspenders. Couldn't stop smiling at the girl who was twirling around in front of him, singing Blondie's "Call Me" woefully out of tune.

I watched them, thinking they looked interesting. They

looked unique. They looked like people who were living the kind of life I wanted.

Before that, I used to go to St. Sebastian's Academy for Young Men, but then my parents decided to blame St. Sebastian's for my brother being gay. So after they kicked Connor out of the house, they sent me to a mixed-gender public school.

You aren't worried he's going to get some girl knocked up? Connor asked my mother at one of our rare family meetings.

I think we'll take our chances, my mother responded, looking wistful, as if my becoming a father at twelve had been an actual possibility. As if the law of averages guaranteed my parents one straight son.

I'm not going and that's that. My father's voice cuts through the walls. Pulling off paint. Dissolving Sheetrock.

But it's Connor's birthday, my mother pleads.

I don't care if it's the Second Coming, my father says. I'm not going to sit in some filthy diner in the godforsaken Village and shove some infected fork in my mouth.

This is the music of our house. This is how things are, now.

Connor and I sit next to each other at a table in Veselka. I try not to stare as he gobbles down meatballs and potato pancakes like he hasn't eaten in a year.

My mother sits on the opposite side of the table from us—if

14

this were a book, my English teacher would label this seating arrangement symbolic—and pushes pierogis around her plate.

Your father is sorry he couldn't make it, Mom says, handing Connor a birthday check. He had to work.

My brother opens his mouth to call Mom out on her obvious lie, but I shake my head, begging him to shut up for once.

And for once, he actually does.

After she pays the bill, Mom hands Connor a slip of paper. Mrs. Jaffe's daughter, Caroline, is moving back to the city, she says, not looking my brother in the eye. You should give her a call.

Connor tilts his head and raises an eyebrow. Waits to see where Mom is going with this.

Well, you were so close when you were kids, she continues, obviously feeling masochistic. And Caroline's such a nice girl.

Connor reaches out to take the paper, looking like a snake ready to gobble up a rat.

In a breathy voice, the deliberately bad Marilyn Monroe impersonation he drags out at parties to make the boys laugh, he says, I don't know, Mom, do you think she'll still let me borrow her high heels?

Then, without another word, he slides out of the booth, tosses the paper behind him, and leaves.

I don't know why your brother has to be so angry all the time, Mom says as we're taking the subway home.

I sometimes forget how good she is at denial. How good

15

she is at forgetting that her inability to stand up to our father had so much to do with Connor moving seven times in four years, crashing on friends' couches and floors. How good she is at pretending she had nothing to do with him working a job for not much more than minimum wage because Dad pulled his college funding.

This time it's *myself* I have to remind to shut up. But it's hard.

Things that fill our house:
→ *My grandmother's old flowered sofas*
→ *A scratching post from our cat, Henry, who died when I was in seventh grade*
→ *Conversations about the weather and the Yankees*
→ *My mother's collection of salt-and-pepper shakers from all fifty states*
→ *My father's anger*
→ *My brother's absence*

It isn't that I'm unhappy, Becks, I say. Not really. It's just that…

Ennui, James interjects, not looking up from the copy of the *New York Times* he's smuggled into our apartment. He has the Arts section spread out across my bedroom floor and is trying to read and solve the crossword at the same time.

Damn, he says, we missed our chance.

What? I ask, happy to have the conversation shifted away from me.

To see the worst play to ever appear on Broadway, James replies. *That* could have made for a good time.

Yeah, well, better not let my dad see that paper, I warn. You know my father only reads the *Post*.

James smirks. He isn't a fan of my father, and I think my dad is scared shitless of him, because James is a walking billboard for everything Dad hates. James looks up at me and says, Seriously, you just need something to be excited about.

I lower my eyes while Becky asks him, Are you *sure* you don't know anyone you can fix Michael up with?

I don't know why Becky thinks that's the answer; for some reason, people in relationships always think that relationships can solve everything.

No, kitten, James says with a sideways glance at me. I'm pretty certain that Michael wouldn't be interested in anyone *I* know.

Well, I guess you could always get a job, she says to me as she gets up to flip the Ramones cassette she's playing to get under James's skin.

Or a dog.

Or a hobby.

Or.

I stare at my guitar.

My guitar stares back.

When Connor was still living here, I played all the time. Filling the nights, drowning out the sounds of my parents' fights, beating down the silence of the house while we all waited to see if my brother was going to come home from wherever it was he'd gone. I played until my fingers bled, until calluses formed, until I was better than I ever thought I could be.

Then Connor got kicked out, and I stopped playing for a while because I didn't want to join a band, and I wasn't sure of my voice, and my father kept telling me to shut the hell up because without all the noise Connor made, the neighbors could hear, and who did I think I was anyhow? John Lennon? Because he was damned if I was going to turn into one of those lipsticked, eye-shadowed, black-wearing weirdos who hung around on St. Mark's looking like they were dead.

My father sells insurance and hates every minute of it.

My father is angry that it's only money from my mother's parents that allowed us to move from Queens to Manhattan.

My father hates that Little Italy is being taken over by Chinatown, but he won't spend any time there because he doesn't want to ride the subway downtown with "all the crazy tourists."

My father has gotten meaner as I've gotten older. Or maybe I'm more aware of it now.

My father plays poker on the first Thursday of every month. He treks to Queens, picking up a six-pack or a bottle of whiskey on the way and doesn't come back until late.

Sometimes he wins money and brings my mother a cake from the Greek bakery she likes. Sometimes he loses money and wakes me by slamming the pantry door too loudly, or drunkenly ranting under his breath about the "damned foreigners" on the 7 train.

But while he's gone, the apartment is quiet, peaceful, relaxed. Mom and I can use the phone without worrying that we'll say the wrong thing. Instead of the TV, Mom will put on music and read or bake or simply hang out.

I leave my bedroom door open on these nights, not worried about being told that I'm a disgrace.

Friday afternoon there's enough snow to close businesses and schools. Seven inches and still falling. My parents wander through the house, unsure of how to interact in daylight when they're both stuck at home.

I'm going out, James says on the other end of the phone.

Out where?

Into the world. Come with me.

I hang up. Pick up the receiver again. Wait for the tone. Dial. Let it ring twice. Hang up.

Miracle; it rings back. I pick up.

You're going to owe me, Connor says instead of hello.

Put it on my tab, I answer, making sure he can hear the sarcasm in my voice.

I throw some gel in my hair, grab my coat, and tell my parents that Connor is working and I have to walk his dog. Which I would do, I think, if he had a dog, because I don't trust my brother to stay home often enough to keep another creature alive.

Maybe I'll crash there so I don't have to deal with the snow, I say.

Mom smiles, happy that Connor and I are close enough that I'd head out in a storm to walk his dog. It's odd, my mother's smile. It isn't the smile of a mother who allowed her son to be kicked out of the house. It's the smile of a mother content with things that don't really exist. She lives in a strange kind of world where Connor is straight and an executive at a bank or a successful filmmaker or a hotshot journalist, anything instead of what he is, a gay shop clerk with more friends than she'll ever have, and a taste for free will.

On the other hand, my father's emotions are written all over his face. The grimace he wears now is the one he always has when I mention Connor. The one he filled the house with, along with his rage, the night Connor graduated from high school and came out to my parents, St. Sebastian's, and all of the Upper West Side as he accepted his diploma, high as a kite, and announced his unfortunately short-lived love for Tony Ramos.

Even now, I can't meet my father's eyes. While he won't go as far as forbidding me from seeing Connor, he makes his feelings clear. I'm not sure if he's more worried that I'm lying about going to my brother's or telling the truth, and he's too afraid of my answer to ask directly. Afraid I might confess to being "that way" too.

In truth, Connor wouldn't need me to walk his dog, he'd probably have friends lining up to do it.

Connor has a knack for collecting people. He meets them at clubs, and in stores, at parties and shows. He strikes up conversations with bartenders and librarians, taxi drivers and street performers. Connor lives his life out loud, but until that night at graduation, I hadn't really noticed *how loud*, and even though it's been four years, the reverb is deafening.

You have to take control of your life and run with it, Connor tells me. Don't let anyone hold you back. There's a world waiting for you. It's big and flashy and exciting, and you need to put yourself out there and grab it. Or let it grab you, you know, whatever you're into.

And while he talks, I can picture it. This community, this family he's replaced us with. These people who can dance all night fueled by rhythm and freedom, drugs and each other. These people who have grabbed their lives away from everyone who has told them they're wrong and they can't and they're damaged. These people who have made themselves into who they want to be, even if it's just for one night.

These people who are not me. Not yet, anyhow.

I don't know if I'm jealous of Connor or of the people he hangs out with. I only know that my brother has moved on to someplace I'm not.

I miss him.

I make my way to James's apartment. He's two years older than me, went to at least three schools I know of, and none could keep him interested enough to show up for anything more than tests. Tests that he passed with honors, but still. Even those weren't enough to make the schools happy. There were meetings with his parents, and meetings with expensive private tutors, and meetings with the psychologists who accused him of acting out. All those meetings never changed anything; James was still James. In the end, each of the schools decided that he might be better suited "elsewhere."

He got his GED, and now his parents, who moved to a sprawling mansion on the water in Connecticut, think he's attending NYU. They deposit his "tuition" into a bank account in the city, out of which he draws a seemingly always-available allowance.

James has made a name for himself in the underground world of performance art and lives in a Hell's Kitchen rent-stabilized share: four guys in three rooms and a snake named Boris in the tub.

Snakes aren't my thing, James told me when he moved in, but at least we'll never have to worry about rats.

The buzzer to James's building is busted, so when I get there, I call up from the pay phone outside the bodega across the street. A cat weaves its way through the fruit display, one bitten ear twitching against the snow, tail dusting a frozen pyramid of apples.

James picks up the phone, and I have to scream over the sound of trumpets and bongos leaking, along with a stream of pot smoke, out of a car window at the stoplight next to the phone booth.

Let me in.

What?

Let me in.

Michael?

The car pulls away.

Let me in.

Oh, why didn't you say that?

I shrug, even though James can't see me.

I wait for James in the vestibule.

This is poetic snow, he says, running down the stairs, wrapping an impossibly long scarf around his neck, It hasn't had time to become tabloid slush.

Connor gave me a fake ID last year for my birthday. I only wanted it so I could get into this club, The Echo. Regardless of what the ID says, I won't be legal to drink for three years, but that's beside the point anyhow, because I wanted to go there to dance, not to get drunk. Even before then, the bouncer, Freddy, had to know I was underage, but New York is sticky hot in summer, and really, what did he care if one more I'm-queer-but-nobody-really-knows-it kid added his sweat to the already wet brick walls of the basement club?

Now, I don't need to wait in line to get in, and they don't ask to see my ID. I love The Echo. If I wanted to, I could be anyone in there. A playboy. A hard-ass. A romantic. I could be a drag queen if I learned to walk in heels.

I could even be myself, if I ever figure out who that is.

Danni is DJing tonight, which means the music is so loud the words are getting sucked into the bass. It's too loud to talk, too loud to hear, too loud to think.

Just the way I like it.

I stare into the spinning blue lights and then blink so that blue spots cover the dark walls, the dark boys, the black jeans, the clear glass, the stretched white shirts.

I'm struck with a sudden and deep hunger. I want it. I want it all.

Relax, the speaker screams. Don't do it.

Easy for Frankie to say.

Over the course of the evening, I:
- → *Dance with a hundred cute shirtless boys*
- → *Sing along to a hundred different songs*
- → *Dream a hundred different dreams*

But at the end of the night, I'm still alone.

James doesn't dance. Instead, he leans against the wall, smoking the long, thin cigarettes he encases in an etched silver holder, his extensive bangs obscuring his face.

Becky says that James observes people like a scientist. I think he's more like an alien, sent to report back to his home planet on the deteriorating state of humanity.

Becky and I have spent an absurd amount of time debating this.

But there's no debate about how tonight will play out. It's always the same.

At some point, almost everyone will try to get James to dance. They'll stand, hand against the wall next to his head, leaning in to make their case. Trying to be charming enough. Sexy enough. Eccentric enough.

James will smile and run his fingers through his hair. For a moment, he'll give them 100 percent of his attention and 90 percent of his piercing gaze, and they'll each feel as if they're the center of his world.

But he won't leave the space he's staked out against the wall. Not until the last song, anyhow.

Then, Danni will give in to James's standing request and play Roxy Music's "More Than This." James will make his way to me, and we'll dance, him swaying like he's possessed, and mouthing the words as Bryan Ferry sings about being carefree for a while.

Everyone will watch. And it's easy to believe, in that moment, there is nothing that matters to him more than that.

Time moves faster as you get older. That's what my dad complains about, anyhow.

I once tried to explain to him how time stretches and retracts on the dance floor. How you can lose yourself in the overlapping beats as one song bleeds into another, and you can almost ride the lights as they swirl and spin, and the smoke of the dry ice mixes with the heady scent of cloves and who knows what else until you're someplace different altogether.

All I got from my father in response was an eye twitch that too closely resembled the one I remember from when Connor still lived at home. I stopped trying to explain it.

Two in the morning comes out of nowhere. James and I stumble onto the street. Ears ringing with silence. Legs adjusting to the tedious movement of walking. Shoulders pressing together for warmth. And snow. Snow everywhere. Piles and piles of it covering the statue of George Washington on his horse in Union Square and still falling.

Before George married Martha, he was in love with his best friend's wife, James tells me, his breath crystalizing in the frigid air.

These are the types of things that James knows. Obscure facts about George Washington. Statistics of sports he doesn't follow. City death tolls from GRID (gay-related immune deficiency), which James tells me is now called AIDS (acquired immune deficiency syndrome), because being gay doesn't equal being dead, and because there is something drastically wrong with naming a disease something that places the blame on those it infects. From what James says, it didn't matter anyhow; the name change hasn't altered anything else.

People are dying regardless.

I guess, given everything, I'd rather hear about George.

Once I asked James why he was so fascinated by other people's relationships.

It's less messy than being in one myself, he said.

Hey! You two want this?

A guy in his twenties, wearing a suit and tie and carrying a fridge door stops near Broadway. The door is clean. Gleaming white as if he'd just ripped it off a floor model at the Appliance Warehouse out on Long Island.

I feel for the five bucks stuffed into the front pocket of my jeans. Mug Money, my mother calls it. Something to give a thief so they don't get your wallet, or your watch, or whatever else you have that's actually worth something.

I've never had to use the fiver and wonder if we're really going to get mugged or if this guy is simply hopped-up on drugs. I mean, why else would he be walking down 17th carrying a fridge door?

I take a step closer to James. He isn't much good in a fight, but he can talk his way out of almost anything. That boy could charm the birds out of the trees, my mother says of James, despite the fact that James is exactly the kind of person my dad thinks is ruining the world. Not that Mom would ever defend James, or anyone, to my dad. Instead, she feeds James. Lasagna. Spaghetti. Cannoli. It's not good to be so thin, she tells him.

The fridge guy breaks into a smile and points at the snow-covered street. I've been sledding all night on it, he says, nodding toward the door. But I can't feel my fingers anymore. It's yours if you want it.

James looks at me and raises an eyebrow. Snowflakes perch on his long lashes, and time shudders to a standstill, leaving me breathless with longing for something…someone…I'll never have. It's as much of a rush as it is painful, like a brain freeze after eating your favorite ice cream. It's a song that craves to be sung, a chord bent out of shape. My feelings for James are just one more of the things I've learned to stay silent about.

It's ultimately pointless anyway.

James shakes his head, sending the snowflakes flying, and time jolts forward. The next thing I know, we're sliding down

Broadway. Careening into curbs and piles of snow. Pushing our-selves off parked cars, holding onto the door, and each other, and our coats. James's scarf wraps around my neck like the last Dr. Who, and James is laughing, laughing, laughing, and I real-ize I've never heard him laugh quite like that before.

Then we slam into a fire hydrant. We're fine, but the door is banged up. So we shake ourselves off, haul it to the sidewalk, and leave it for someone else to salvage.

We walk crosstown. The trip takes three times as long as normal because of the snow and because James insisted on wearing boots with metal heels instead of anything remotely practical. By the time we get to his apartment, we're both shaking with cold. James jimmies the lock on the front door while I stand guard. Last week, someone was stabbed in the tiny lobby.

You sure there's room for me? I ask, wheezing like a pack-a-day smoker as we hike up five floors of stairs.

In front of me, James shrugs. There's always room for you, Michael, you know that. Besides, he says, slowing down so much I almost run into him, we're one person down. Steven is in the hospital.

Oh no. What happened?

We reach the top floor, James pulls open the door, and we huddle inside. He stops again before he says, Pneumonia, I think. His sister came and cleared out his stuff.

I wait for some bit of random information, the dosage of a common antibiotic shot or Steven's third cousin's middle name, but James is quiet, staring at the couch.

I stop short of asking whether they'd cleaned the cushions. It doesn't matter. Not like I'm going to make it home in this weather.

James's roommates:

There's Rob, who almost got arrested with James at a rally to save some Broadway theaters from being torn down last year. There's Ted, who is a painter. James thinks Ted's father owns the apartment, but isn't sure since Ted doesn't talk much and James sends his rent check to some P.O. box in the Bronx. Then there's Steven, who does lighting or something and travels a lot and has the couch in the front room.

Had, I guess.

Most of the guys who have lived here are older, somewhere in their mid to late twenties, with jobs as waiters or cashiers they never talk about, and dreams of being actors or musicians that obsess them.

When I'm here and they're talking about art and meaning and rehearsals and their big breaks, I want to be one of them.

Only later do the doubts creep in. Only later do I remember the late notices from the electric company stuck to the fridge door and the drunks passed out in the doorway.

Only later do I wonder what's really going on with Steven.

Some are saying seventeen inches, some twenty-four. Either way, it's a lot of snow. The subway is running because it's easier, apparently, to keep it going than to shut it off and restart it. We can go anywhere we want, except it's the middle of the night and we're in Hell's Kitchen and there's nowhere to go.

Smoke leaks out from under Ted's door.

The ceiling squeaks like it's going to come down. Rob pounds on it with a broom and says, Fucking newlyweds. Then he shakes his head and laughs at the double meaning of his own joke.

We hang out in the living room. I try to solve a Rubik's Cube. Blue. Red. Yellow. Nope, the green and white are wrong. Start again.

James sits on the floor, leaning against the wall, legs folded insect-like, smoking the thin cigarettes he rolls himself.

James is a collection of straight lines. His concave cheekbones and his too-straight nose, the cut of his cream-colored hair, the lapels on his jacket decorated with ever-changing pins of silver crowns, ringed hands, tiny bells.

My edges are round. My hair curls violently when it's wet. James's waist-cinched jackets are too restrictive for me to dance in. And mostly that's okay. But there are nights when I watch James, and his straight lines, and his straight fingers around a straight cigarette, and I wish I were more like him.

Rob likes to flirt.

And he likes to flirt with me, although we both know it's a joke.

But James isn't the only one in the apartment who seems

30

subdued tonight. Everyone is kind of glancing at the couch and then looking away without saying anything.

Rob is stretched out perpendicular to me, his long legs on top of mine, back on the floor, eyes on the smoke that rises toward the ceiling.

Oh, Michael, Michael, Michael, he says, dramatically breaking the silence. Why don't you have a boyfriend?

All of James's roommates are dramatic. And I don't know them well enough to tell what's real and what's theater, or to know whether I should even care.

Maybe I have a boyfriend and I just haven't told you, I tease back.

As if.

I stare at the laces on Rob's shoes. They're blue. Faded.

And easier to look at than James's face when I'm lying about having a boyfriend.

MTV is blaring in one of the bedrooms. *I Want My MTV*, a variety of rock stars chant.

I kind of wish I could see it, because watching MTV at home around my dad is risking a lecture on morality and, of all things, fashion.

As if either of those were things my dad knew anything about.

I assumed I'd sleep on Steven's vacated couch, but am not about to put up a fight when James suggests the beanbag chair in his room instead.

Do you think Steven will be okay? I ask, Is he coming back?

James shrugs a sad I-don't-want-to-talk-about-it shrug. I don't know what he's hiding or whether I'd want to hear it, but I'm not going to press.

I follow him to his room, a world away from the rest of the apartment.

Tapestries from India line the walls.

A stack of Playbills threatens to topple over on his tiny desk.

A Styrofoam head wears a pair of shutter shades.

His cologne, spicy and intoxicating, fills the room.

James lights two oil lamps that hang from the wall as I settle in on the beanbag at the side of his twin bed.

Every time I move, it sounds like one of those rain sticks they sell in the Village. Like James's laugh while we were riding the fridge door.

We talk about music, whether film can ever be considered as much of an art form as live theater, and the rumor about a new Bowie album, until we're hoarse and James is tired enough to allow the British accent he inherited from his mother to bleed through.

I've been hired to collaborate on a new performance piece, he says.

Then James tells me he wants me to contribute sound to it. Not, he explains, music, but noises. Guitar strings breaking. A percussive effect. A chord out of tune.

Out of tune? I ask. I spend all my time getting *in* tune.

But aren't all things more interesting if they're ever-so-slightly wrong? James asks.

I shrug. If that were true, I'd be the most interesting guy in the world.

I wake to a clatter of dishes. James is obsessed with breakfast. Somewhere in his past, he had a German nanny, and on weekends he likes to recreate her puffed apple pancakes, piles of bacon strips, fresh squeezed juice.

I make my way to the kitchen, passing Rob who gives me a seductive, sleepy smile that makes me wish I were attracted to guys in their midtwenties with facial hair.

James is quiet as he cooks, measuring flour and who knows what into a large bowl. Duran Duran meets Julia Child, Becky likes to say about him.

It's funny, though. I have a hard time seeing James as Simon Le Bon. Sure, he's got those delicate features and his hair is cut in kind of the same way, but James always makes me feel like he's going to morph into something else. Something dark and slightly dangerous. I told him that once, curious to hear his response. He just smiled.

As if she's been summoned by my thinking about her, Becky calls.

James holds out the phone to me.

Becky says, Your mom told me you were at Connor's, so I figured you were at James's. Meet me at the cathedral?

Becky is pretty much Jewish. Technically, half. Or maybe a quarter. Her family is as much a melting pot as the city, and people are always looking at her permanently tanned skin and her dark straight hair that she's constantly teasing, and her dark blue eyes, and asking her where she's from as if "here" isn't an option.

Anyhow, her dad was the only one who practiced. Now

he's gone, and her mom doesn't care about religion. Though she still goes to a synagogue on the big holidays, standing in the back because she doesn't have a ticket, somewhere along the line Becky has become fascinated with Catholic churches: the incense, the music, the candles, the stained glass. She doesn't go to mass; it isn't about worship, she tells me. She only likes to pop in at odd times, when she has St. Patrick's mostly to herself. She says she likes to hear her steps echo through the high arches.

I cock my eyebrow at James, who is taking off a yellow apron. He knows what she's asking without my having to repeat it.

Tell God I said hello, he says. James tries to avoid religion at all costs.

I'm somewhere in between. Catholic school years aside, I'm not particularly interested in religion, but not totally ready to rule it out yet either. Plus, I'm kinda pissed at my dad for using God as an excuse to kick Connor out of the house. As if my dad has any use for God. Or God has any obvious use for him.

Come, I mouth to James, silently begging. Sometimes church makes Becky depressed and I'm already feeling out of sorts.

James holds out his hand for the phone and passes me the apron in trade.

I love you to pieces, kitten, he says into the phone, but it's you and Michael today.

Damn.

They talk about the snow for a while, and when he hangs up, his hand stays on the receiver, back in its cradle.

I want to ask him if he's okay. He has these moments with

34

Becky sometimes, like there's something he wants to say but can't, and they seem to be happening more and more lately.

But then he turns, that sly smile on his face, and says, Light a candle for me, will you?

I need to learn to say no. Becky tells me that all the time; only she never wants me to say no to *her*.

When I walk into the church after trudging through the snow for what feels like an hour, she says, You're late, you missed the bells.

The bells. Of course. Becky knows facts about the bells— even their names—the same way James knows facts about... everything.

It's snowing, I remind her. You know, like a lot.

She bumps her shoulder into mine, surrounding us in a cloud of powdery perfume. A dusting of slush sprays off my coat.

No shit, Sherlock, she says with a laugh. But you still missed the bells.

I offer my apology, though, really, I'm surprised I made it at all.

Did you get home okay last night? I ask. Becky lives in Queens but lies and uses her aunt's address on the Upper West Side, so she can go to our school in Manhattan. Her aunt actually lives in California, though, and only rents the place out, so it isn't like Becky can move there for real or anything.

I crashed at Andy's, she says, And don't look at me like that. His mom took the night shift at St. Vincent's, but his dad was there.

Andy's mom is a nurse and his dad is, like, seven-feet tall and a cop who no doubt made Andy sleep on the couch and kept his hand on the butt of his gun all night.

So remind me why your boyfriend doesn't do this church thing with you again?

Becky snorts. He doesn't believe in God.

And you're Jewish, I say. So why go to church?

She smiles, and in the light that's shining through the stained glass, she looks a little angelic.

I believe in an equal opportunity God, she says. Sue me. Come on, let's light some candles.

I always feel pressured lighting candles in church. If I light one for one of my grandparents, I worry the other might feel slighted. What if I light one for a cousin and forget someone else?

Then there's James. It's kind of odd lighting candles for people who are alive, right? I ask Becky, even though, lapsed as I am, I'm the one who should know. But I feel as though I'm jinxing people when I light one in their name. Like it's some sort of bad omen.

It's fine, Michael, she says, slipping a couple of dollars into the box. It's about intention and prayer.

Intention?

What if my intentions and James's are different?

I can't lie in church, not even to myself, so I switch my focus to prayer.

What would James want me to pray for?

Why don't I know?

Be happy, I think as I light a candle for him. And even though Becky thinks it's okay, I still feel weird about doing it.

But he asked.

That being said, Becky might be on to something. I feel lighter as I leave the church. Like I've done something worthwhile.

It's still snowing. *Still snowing*. And since it isn't ridiculously cold, I walk back home, notes flying through my head. They'd make a good song if I'd only remember them, which I won't.

I'm sleep-drunk. Or rather, tired-drunk. Exhausted. And the snow is making me numb and giddy. Happy. And that's the odd thing. Not being happy, but realizing it. Because how often, when you're happy, do you have the chance to step back and notice?

When the snow clears, the city goes back to trying to clean up the subway cars. Monday, they take the 1 train out of service, and on Tuesday, it comes back silver and heartless. It's as if they dipped the whole thing in peroxide, and I spend the whole ride trying not to touch anything.

By Wednesday, the train is comfortably covered in tags and graffiti again, the station boasting a Haring chalk drawing of dancing figures losing themselves in joy.

My morning starts with chemistry.

How's your brother? Mrs. Bryson asks. She had him his

senior year and really liked him, even tutoring him for free to get his grades up high enough for college applications.

He's good, I say, not knowing if I'm telling the truth. I have to assume Connor's good since it isn't like he's easy to get hold of. But at least he's having fun, I guess.

Is he giving any thought to college? she asks.

Mrs. Bryson knows that my dad cut Connor off financially after kicking him out of the house, so he had to get a job. But no way am I telling her that I'm pretty sure his entire hourly salary goes toward boys and drugs and summer tickets for the ferry to Fire Island.

Whatever he's giving thought to, I doubt it has much to do with school.

I have study hall third period, but nothing to study for. Instead, I smuggle my UK single of U2's "New Year's Day," which was totally worth getting since it came with an extra 45 of three live tracks, into one of the language labs that line the back wall of the library. Then I shut the door, and hope the librarians won't do a spot check.

I put the disc on the turntable, grab the worn headphones, and mouth the words to the songs, hoping that anyone passing will think I'm conjugating French verbs. Which I'm not.

Then I read the wall. The story goes that some kids started writing on the walls of the lab back in the seventies. Things like: *Even though I'm in ROTC, I don't support this war,* and *I'm not sure how to feel about my brother getting out of serving in Vietnam by wearing woman's underwear to his draft meeting.*

Now, there's paper covering the marked-up wood, and everyone refers to this as the "fear room." Now, it says things like, *I missed a period and I'm afraid I'm pregnant* and *They're calling this thing the gay plague, and I wonder if having sex is going to kill me.*

As Bono sings about blood-red skies, I grab a pen, and under the last comment, I write, *Me too.*

I don't sit around thinking about the fact that I'm attracted to boys, because then I start thinking about all the things I want and don't know how to get.

And I don't talk about the fact that I'm attracted to boys because I don't see the point, given that I obviously don't have a boyfriend or anything, and the only reason I have somewhere to live is because, having heard nothing to the contrary, my parents assume I'm straight.

Besides, Connor has done enough talking for both of us.

I try to have dinner with Connor on Wednesday nights, but it doesn't always happen. He's cancelled so often that I'm surprised when he actually shows up.

This week, he's actually at the diner before me, wearing a black tux jacket over a gray T-shirt that's probably supposed to be white. The block letters on the shirt say SAVE THE FUTURE.

Connor works at a thrift store in the West Village. He sorts the clothes when they come in and keeps a lot of the best stuff for himself.

He sticks his foot out—he's wearing black-and-white saddle shoes—and says, Maurice.

I stare at him. Then I ask, You've named your shoes?

He hits me on the arm with the menu, and says, No, idiot. The designer. Maurice.

I stare at him some more until he shakes his head. You're hopeless, he says. Do you know how much these would go for at Charivari? I got them for a steal. I can't believe anyone would throw them out.

When I keep staring at him, wondering how anyone could get so amped about footwear, he says, You know nothing about the world outside of Mom and Dad's. The thing is, you won't learn anything about life until you move out on your own. I have a futon waiting for you. I'll even get it cleaned. And you can have your friends over. Or, you know, whatever.

I don't point out that not knowing the name of a designer doesn't mean I have no life.

I get that Connor doesn't understand why I don't follow in his footsteps, tell Dad to shove it, get myself thrown out. So I also don't point out that he isn't even listed on the lease of the place where he's living and could get evicted at any minute.

Why would I want that for myself?

Why would he?

But realizing that makes me feel sorry for him. My brother lives in the moment. I have no clue how it would feel to be that carefree or how he manages to ignore all the shitty stuff that's happened to him. He must take after Mom.

So, knowing I might regret it, I ask if he wants to come with me to Echo on Friday. Connor might be almost five years older than me, but he still doesn't have his shit together, regardless of what he thinks.

A complicated expression flashes across his face. The same one he wore at St. Sebastian's on Christmas Eve, and I think, for a minute, he might say yes.

But then he glances away, smirks, and says, That's your scene, not mine. I don't need to jump up and down in front of a roomful of coked-up boys to get laid.

I swallow an equally snotty comeback because I can't win when he's like this.

I know he'd rather hang out with his friends and screw around at the baths or on the street or wherever else he thinks his next high or fuck will come from. There's no way that spending time with his little brother can touch that.

I think back to the writing on the wall of the fear room. Just be careful, I say so quietly there's no chance of him hearing. Not like he'd pay attention anyhow.

James tells me to take Connor up on his offer to crash with him. James tells me spending the next year at my parents' before going to college is going to hurt my song writing. James tells me he knows a girl who knows a girl who can get me on the bill at The Bitter End. James tells me he smoked the best joint of his life last week. James tells me if I moved out, I could go dancing every night and just forget, forget, forget.

FEBRUARY 1983

Make sure you finish your homework at lunch so that you can
come with me tonight, my dad says.

There was a time when my father would invite me to come
with him to ball games and work barbeques, to spend Saturdays
with him in the office, and even once to join him at the bar
with his buddies.

But that was a long, long time ago.

Come with you where? I ask, without thinking. Before he
can answer, I have a flash of memory. Connor going with him
to his poker game and coming home with a perfect imprint of
my father's hand on his arm.

Alan's son has been joining us, he says. You two can hang out together.

Alan works at the insurance office with my father. I've met his son before and have no reason to ever do it again.

I have a chemistry test to study for, I say. And I suck at poker, remember? You used to say you didn't want me to come along and embarrass you.

My father sighs and walks away. He'll do anything to avoid being embarrassed around "the guys." I've dodged a bullet this time.

There used to be a time when Connor and I both wanted to go with him, just to see what happened on these mysterious jaunts to Queens. But that was before we understood the type of people our dad called friends. Before we understood that we were the enemy.

Where's Andy? James asks Becky. I think he's trying to torture her or make her realize they should break up or something.

James and Becky are always trying to get under each other's skin, but something about this topic makes me squirm, because while Andy and James are polar opposites, Andy is a good guy and as long as he makes Becky happy, I think we should be happy for them.

It's like James is penalizing her for being the only one of us in a relationship.

Becky looks up and answers, On patrol. Like always.

James makes a point of not looking at me when he says, Well, there *are* other boys. Other girls. Other…

I'm sure she knows that, I cut him off.

44

James doesn't like to think about my sordid past, she says.

Like he's one to talk, I joke.

James rolls his eyes and says, Oh, you'd be surprised.

Later, I wrap the phone cord around my wrist like a snake.

So how wild is your past, Becks? I tease. I've heard rumors and all that, but it's not like I really believe them.

Oh, you know, she says. Before I met Andy…well, I've always liked falling in love more than being in a relationship.

I nod, even though she can't see me. Even though I'm not sure what it's like to really fall in love or to be in a relationship. Or which I'd like better.

I pull the cord tight around my wrist, oddly enjoying the way my fingers go cold and numb.

But, she says, and I can hear her pause, figuring out the best way to string together her words. She settles on, Let's talk about James. Can you name anyone he's actually been with?

Becky's theory confuses me because James is always surrounded by girls, always surrounded by boys. Always in the center of a storm of admirers. Who knows what he does when he isn't with us? And when would he have time to get to know one person and why would he bother?

But no, I tell her. I don't know anyone.

Me either, she says. And don't you think that's strange?

It's just James, I answer. It's like the way he taps on the top of a pack of cigarettes for luck before he opens them. Or the way he goes to dance clubs but won't dance.

There's a pause while I try to picture James in a relationship, going on dates, too busy on Friday nights to go to rehearsal or develop a new show. Uninspired.

I listen to Becky breathe out before she says, Yeah, or he's hooked on someone he already knows.

I've heard this theory from her before.

And it still makes my heart race in an uncomfortable way.

Regardless of what Becky thinks. Regardless of how I always feel a little happier, a little more energized around him, James Barrows is out of my league. And regardless of the fact that he probably spends more time with me than anyone, there's no way he's hooked on me as anything other than his best friend.

'Night, Becks, I say and unravel the phone cord. It leaves a red mark around my wrist, shaped like barbed wire.

It's Valentine's Day and the girls from Student Council interrupt Mr. Solomon's class. They're weighed down with carnations for their fund-raiser. Red. White. Pink. The colors match the girls' shirts and their lip gloss and the oversized bows in their oversized hair.

A garden's worth of flowers land on a classroom's worth of desks. Two, one white, one pink, land in front of me. The white one first from Becky. The card reads: *Pretend this is from the future and signed by your one true love.*

The pink one is also in Becky's handwriting. *James gave me a Kennedy half dollar to send this to you. Make of that what you will.*

Sometimes it's like this: I can stay in my room with my books and my music and my guitar and my dreams, and stare out the window and be content.

Leaving means opening the door and heading down the hall and dealing with the looks and the silences and the questions— Where are you going, Michael? and Is that eye makeup? You aren't turning into a fag like your brother, are you?—and the glares and the anger, and sometimes it's just easier to stay in my room.

But sometimes it isn't. Sometimes it's worth the abuse.

The Echo is crowded. Everyone freed from their snow caves.

I sip a Coke and watch until I can't resist the pull of the music. Then I dance. And I dance. Waiting for that feeling of losing myself in something. Becoming something. Something that isn't me. Something more.

There's a boy in black watching me. We're all in black, but there's something darker about him, something even more than a typical Goth. He sways off tempo, like he can't quite find the beat, his red eyes ringed with kohl against a drug-pale face that would be impossible to imagine breaking into a smile.

I try not to stare back. Try and fail. He's captivating in the same way as a gun, in the same way as the stained knife that Andy found last month on patrol. The boy is wearing a crop top under a wool coat far too warm to dance in. His emaciated ribs jut out every time he moves.

He comes over and stands too close. Head cocked at an odd angle, the dark centers of his eyes, planet-like. I wonder what he's on.

47

You should come home with me, he says, under his breath, under the music.

I almost laugh because I'm not the kind of guy that people say things like this to. But I look at the boy and his eyes flare with something like anger or hunger, and I wonder if this is how James feels being hit on all the time and why he doesn't get involved.

Thanks, but...

He leans in, breath hot on my neck. We live in Brooklyn, he says. We have a coven. We would love you.

I swallow hard and pull back.

No, I say. I'm good.

Figures. The only ones I can attract are nuts.

He extends his middle finger as I turn and walk away. Apparently, drugged-out Brooklyn vampires can't handle rejection.

This week when I see Connor, I try to keep things light. Usually I drone on about Mom and Dad, and all the things he's missing at home, which takes massive creativity on my part and usually revolves around food and space, and abundant hot water, because really, what else is there?

This week, I let my brother do all the talking. Connor tells me he's seeing a drag queen whose stage name is Destiny, but whose day job is in advertising, which really means he sells classifieds for *The Daily News*. But, Connor says, it's an honest living. They've been meeting every night, but Destiny won't go back to his apartment because it's a fifth floor walk-up and he doesn't want to work that hard. Not for my brother, anyway.

I look at Connor, sure he's lying, but it's hard to tell about which part.

When we get up to leave, I grab a plastic bag off the seat and hand it to Connor. *I <3 NY* the bag declares, but I'm pretty sure it wasn't designed by someone handing off bread, peanut butter, and the occasional fiver he's saved from his allowance to his older brother.

I know Connor's working, but I don't think food is at the top of his shopping list.

And I know he hates this part because he never says anything, not even thanks.

But he never refuses the bag either, and I guess that's something.

MARCH 1983

Have you read this?

James tosses a newspaper at me. The *New York Native*. Even though we're in my room, with the door shut, and my father is at work, and I know it would take him forty minutes to get here if the subways are running on time and he walks faster than normal and doesn't stop on the way home for a drink or anything, the thought of how he'd react to finding a gay newspaper in my room makes me break out in a cold sweat.

James...

Read, he says. I'll throw it in the bin on the corner when I leave.

The article is bylined "Larry Kramer" and it's filled with numbers and fear. Just the kind of things James collects.

1,112. The current number of AIDS cases.

418. The number of dead already this year. And it's only March.

47.6. The percentage of infected cases who live in New York.

3 years. Life expectancy.

I read the article. The facts. The anger. The call to action. The cataloging of the things that haven't been done.

My shoulders tense thinking of what it could mean.

But James, I haven't, I say, and then stop because for all that we've talked about—despite the fact that James knows me better than anyone—we've never directly discussed our sex lives. Or in my case, my lack of one.

He grabs the paper from me and points to this:

> *No matter what you've heard, there is no single profile for all AIDS victims. There are drug users and non-drug users. There are the truly promiscuous and the almost monogamous. There are reported cases of single-contact infection.*
>
> *All it seems to take is the one wrong fuck. That's not promiscuity—that's bad luck.*

Oh.

So no one is ever supposed to have sex again?

Where the hell does that leave me?

Where does that leave any of us?

Third period and I'm back in the fear room, even though I forgot to bring an album or something to make it look like I have a reason to be here.

The same paper is up as last time. *I kissed my best friend's brother,* one new note reads in purple ink. The "gay plague" note is still there, as is my response. Under that are two comments. I disregard the scrawled, *Get a room,* but the other, in the same ink as the first, says, *It's like, what's the point, you know? Why deal with assholes like this ^ and the chance of getting the shit kicked out of you just for walking down the street and maybe getting thrown out of your house, and still be too afraid to get laid because no one knows what's causing this damned thing?*

Have to admit, the author has a point. I wonder if he's read the article in the *Native* and what he'd think about it.

James is finishing a show.

There is always a show being written, cast, rehearsed. Opening, closing.

Becky and I try to keep track, but I sometimes think that James doesn't tell us about all of his work. And I sometimes think that's a good thing.

The questions don't quit:

Are you going to college?

Getting a job?

Volunteering for the Peace Corps?

What are you going to do with your life?

What are you going to do?

WHAT ARE YOU GOING TO DO???

I should help Mom steam the wallpaper off Connor's old room so that she can use the space for exercise or sewing or something more than storage, given that it's been almost four years.

I should be writing a paper on Chaucer.

I should storm into the living room and confront my father for kicking Connor out and convince him he's been a dick.

I should convince Connor to…I don't know what. Move home? Not like that's going to happen. And really, I can't blame him, even though I want to.

I should grab my guitar and learn the melody line to "New Year's Day," even though the really cool stuff is in the bass part.

I'm jittery. All nervous energy and potential.

Someone plays a sax on the street and the sound floats over the hum of the city and swaggers through our windows, even though they're closed. My fingers dance to the rhythm. I need to be out. Out. OUT.

I'd like to know where you're getting all this money to throw away, my father says.

He's standing in front of the apartment door, blocking my way, and I can feel my mouth go dry.

I still have a little money from Christmas, I answer honestly, taking into account the money I gave to Connor. But seriously, it's just the price of a subway token and a Coke.

Dad narrows his eyes in a way that makes me feel totally naked, and I wish I could punch something. I look down, glad I've played it safe in dark jeans and a white shirt. Then, remembering, I shake my head slightly, hoping my hair will cover my ear cuff. I've got eyeliner hidden in my jacket pocket, and I'm not stupid enough to put it on until I'm at the club. I wish it didn't feel like Dad could see through the fabric.

I know from experience this standoff will go one of two ways. Either he's in the mood for a fight, in which case I'm screwed. Or he's trying to rattle me, in which case I just need to wait him out.

Maybe you should spend that money on a haircut, he says. You're beginning to look like a fucking girl.

I bite my tongue. Literally. And wait silently. A cop car screams down the street, and our upstairs neighbor must be getting ready to go out too, because I can hear her high heels clack against her wood floors.

Finally, my father sighs, Get out of here already. And don't let me see you coming in past curfew, do you hear me?

Connor would have said: Of course I can hear you; the whole Upper West Side can hear you.

But I know when to keep quiet.

This is only one of the things that makes me smarter than my brother.

The Echo is packed. Sometimes it gets like this. Random people called to the same pulsing beat at exactly the same time.

55

Sometimes I mind. Tonight, I don't. Tonight, I need this mad crush of people and noise.

I dance until I can't walk. Sweat runs down my back. My legs start to ache. My anxiety hunkers down like a dog sleeping in the corner.

I've almost made it to that place where nothing matters.

And then I stop.

It's his eyes that get me. Gray. Or green. Or perhaps, blue. Hard to tell in the flashing lights, but they're big and perfectly rimmed with kohl, and they stand out against his brown skin and his black hair and his white shirt and follow me across the room to where I can no longer dance, but I merely perform.

I'm aware of every beat. Every move of my arms. Every breath.

I try to push that all out of my mind. Synth beats. Smoke. Lights. The scents of cologne and dry ice and alcohol. I open myself up and let it fill me.

Only.

Those.

Eyes.

Suddenly we're dancing together. Not just next to each other, pushed adjacent by the jostling crowd in our black jeans and black eyeliner, but together, mirroring each other's movements, sharing glances.

Three songs later and he's still there, his lopsided smile

telling me he knew that I knew that we were in it for an hour, or at least another song.

All the while I watch him covered with blue dots like stars in a dark sky.

There's a slice of silence as New Order's "Blue Monday" slides into Re-Flex's "The Politics of Dancing."

The boy motions me over to the wall. Away from the people. Far from the speakers.

I've seen you here, he says. Before.

He phrases it like its two sentences. With a pause between "here" and "before." It's difficult not to analyze his comment. He's noticed me in the past enough to recognize me in the present.

While I try to figure out how I can respond—as if I could respond—he adds, With your friend. With James.

Well, of course he'd know James. Everyone at The Echo knows James. The only reason he would notice me is because I was with James.

So I smile and nod, and I wait for the questions to start: What is James really like? Are you seeing him? Is he seeing anyone? Does he like boys or girls? What's his deal, anyhow? Can you give me his number?

This time there are no questions. This time there is only: I've been wanting to meet you. To talk to you. To dance with you. I've been waiting until you were alone.

His name is Gabriel. And all I can think of is the angel.

We talk about the music. We talk about the club and the boys and the girls and the snow and about how sad it was that Karen Carpenter died. We talk about everything and nothing, even when we aren't sure we heard right because of the relentless thump of the bass and the pressing crunch of the dancers and because I keep losing my train of thought while I'm looking into his eyes. Trying to figure out if they're really blue or just blue in the lights.

He never does ask about James.

As we're talking and dancing, I'm also hovering somewhere over the bar, soaring above the room, lost in the lights. Danni throws on Lena Lovich, singing about wanting a new toy. Very funny. I'm not sure who he thinks the toy is, Gabriel or me.

I watch us dance. Watch myself nervously fidget with my favorite blue skinny tie, the one Connor found at the store and put aside because he said the pattern of guitar picks reminded him of me.

Gabriel doesn't fidget. Gabriel dances like fire released. Gabriel moves like someone used to being watched. Someone who likes it.

Gabriel wears his jeans tight and his shirt loose, and I can see him sneaking glances at me as if I'm the type of person that someone like him would sneak glances at.

Lena's voice soars loud, asking what we want.

What do I want?

What am I allowed to want?

The bouncers are selective, yet random. But somehow they always let in the old women who sell cassettes and flowers at the end of the night. Flower for you. Flower for your boyfriend. Flower. Flower. Flower.

Gabriel buys me an indigo-blue rose. To remember me by, he says, and I cringe at the finality in his words.

When he hugs me goodbye, his eyes are as black as a subway tunnel. The rose feels insubstantial in my hands; cold comfort when what I'm yearning for is everything contained in this boy in front of me.

But then he leans in, runs a hand under the edge of my sweaty shirt, up my back, and says, Next week.

Did it happen?

If I close my eyes, I can see Gabriel.

But through the Sunday fog of homework…

And my mother's Run to the store and pick up flour, Michael…

Connor's on the line for you, don't stay on long, your father is expecting a call…

It feels like a dream. *He* feels like a dream.

After my parents are asleep, I call James.

I met someone last night, I whisper.

Tell me.

I tell him about Gabriel's eyes and how he was wearing an earring with a cursive *S* on it, the one I couldn't bring myself to ask about.

I tell James about how he sang along to the songs in perfect pitch and how, when we were talking, he'd duck his head and look at me through his coal-black lashes.

I tell him nothing that matters.

But I tell him and *that* matters.

I tell him "New Toy" is my new favorite song, and he laughs. What do you want?

I don't think I have to answer.

In the morning, my mother sees the flower and asks if it's for her. I can't think up a lie so I say yes.

She transfers it to a bud vase and a few hours later, I have to change the blue-tinged water. I didn't know you were into horticulture, she says, only my tired brain processes it as whore-to-culture and I choke, wondering what she knows. Then she has me get a wet rag to clean up the coffee I spit on her newly cleaned floor.

Becky comes to school on Monday in a hot-pink fishnet shirt and huge gold cross earrings. I bought this shirt from your brother, she tells me. Of course she did, Connor always gives James and Becky his employee discount.

I hope you washed it first, I say. Some of that stuff comes in looking pretty grungy. I don't ask about the earrings.

When we meet up with James after school, he tells me I need to let Connor pick out my clothes next week when I go back to The Echo. Becky tells him to shut up and that I can do fine on my own. He stops talking. She's the only one who can get away with it.

My parents are fighting again. Something about Connor and health insurance and why doesn't he get a real job so he can pay for his own benefits and food and not just his tiny squatter's apartment that he's only living in until his friend or coworker or whatever gets back to town wheneverthehell that is.

I put the pillow over my head and shut my eyes tight until all I can see are blue lights dancing against my lids. Gabriel, I think. Gabriel.

I've never gone to the club two weeks in a row. It's too hard arguing with my parents about curfews, too hard coming up with the money for cover and drinks and transport, too easy to give myself over to the lights and the smoke and the boys. Well, watching them anyway.

Then again, no one has ever asked if I was coming back before, so there's that.

APRIL 1983

James comes over on Friday and reminds me that this week is The Echo's half-year Halloween party. I need to dress up, only I have nothing to wear, and Gabriel will be there, and I think I'm going to be sick.

Wait, he says, I have just the thing. He pulls black jeans and a black shirt from my closet and starts sticking on pieces of a broken mirror that he found in the alley and shoved into his bag somehow knowing, in his James way, that he'd need it at some point.

He says, You'll be a disco ball. Then he shrugs and says, It's the best I can do on short notice.

I'm at the club at nine when the only people there are the bartenders, a couple making out in the corner, and Martin and Pedro. Pedro is a parrot and Martin is a bar regular who likes to wear impossibly high gold-glittered platforms. They make the rounds every weekend because people like to give Pedro beer, but he'll only drink the Mexican stuff. Martin taught him to say "give me another," and so they do. At least until Martin has to take the bird home to sober up.

Sipping a Coke, I dance alone to Yaz.

What are you supposed to be? Brian calls from behind the bar. Seven years of bad luck?

I choke on a piece of ice and a sense of foreboding.

I see Gabriel across the now-crowded room, only I've had too much caffeine and I'm not even sweating it out because the music sucks so I'm not really dancing and I just want to bolt. Maybe he won't see me.

See me.

Please. See me.

Gabriel catches me staring and smiles before I can look away.

James once said that "precipice" was his favorite word and now I know why.

I'm on the edge of something. On the edge and I want to fall. I want to fall so badly.

Gabriel's dark clothes are covered in glow-in-the-dark stars that reflect in the mirrors on my own. I'm night, he tells me. You can be my light.

These are the things I learn about Gabriel: For minimum wage plus tips, he delivers balloons for parties, bar mitzvahs, and weddings. I have to wear this awful red jumpsuit, he says. And you haven't lived until you've had to get into a crowded subway car with three dozen balloons. But it's cool. No one is sad or angry when you're bringing them balloons.

He tells me he used to get good grades, and he used to live in the city, and he used to be a gymnast, and he used to pretend to have a girlfriend. But then his father was killed by some random guy on the F train. Gabriel quit school. He quit the gym. He quit the pretend girlfriend. His mom moved them to the Bronx where they live in a one-bedroom apartment over a smoke shop.

Gabriel decided then that if he had to work to support his mom and little sister, if he had to sleep in a converted closet, he was going to do whatever things he could to make himself happy.

As he's talking, I realize I want to be one of those things.

One of *his* things.

I told Gabriel I live on the Upper West Side, which isn't a lie, but James says I should have made up something more exotic.

I told Gabriel I'm only sixteen, and he laughed and said, Age is only a number. He just turned eighteen, anyhow.

I told him I'd write him a song.

I told him I'd never been kissed, although I can't tell that to anyone anymore.

A kiss should be so simple. Lips against lips.

A fulfillment of the promise I made to myself when I was twelve.

A new promise created.

After Becky and Andy went on their second date, she told me how he'd kissed her in the lobby of the movie theater.

An older woman standing in the bookstore aisle next to us had smiled. Becky didn't care who heard her. She didn't have to.

Gabriel and I hid in the shadows created by the fog and the lights of the dance floor. We weren't hiding from ourselves, but from the world, and everyone who might hate us for it.

Our kiss was a secret we didn't want to keep.

But we had no choice.

As I'm getting ready for bed, a star falls out of my shirt and onto the floor. I place it under my pillow.

I wish. I wish.

I'm too busy wishing to sleep.

When I was ten, I taught myself to play guitar upside down like Paul McCartney plays bass with the strings reversed and everything, because I'm useless doing anything right-handed.

My dad asked why I couldn't play something "manly" like the trumpet and join marching band. I told him I hated football, and he never asked again.

I play through my favorite minor chords. Then the major. I thought that orange was the only word not to rhyme with anything, but Gabriel doesn't seem to rhyme with much either.

From our fourth-floor apartment, the city looks like just a bunch of lights. Streetlamps. Storefronts. Cars. Windows.

Behind each one, a story, I guess.

People fighting and falling in love. People having sex and having doubts.

I want someone to tell me how it happens. Growing up. Finding your place in the world.

The houses and the lovers and the jobs and the thoughts and the drama of it all. How do I make it my own?

The next day, I ask James if he'd consider writing lyrics for a song for me.

Oh, you wouldn't want that.

Wouldn't I?

Lyrics aside, I want my guitar to sound like The Edge, but it always comes out more like Paul Simon.

Flipping through channels at James's before the stations sign off for the night.

Hey, look, he says, nodding toward the TV. He comes back to sit on the couch. Taps on the top of a cigarette pack. Puts it down.

I don't really have to. I've seen this before. David Bowie on an old *Saturday Night Live* rerun from the seventies. He's wearing a blue dress and heels like a stewardess, and, behind him one of the singers, a performance artist James likes, named Joey Arias, wears matching red, right down to his hair.

But I know who has James's attention. Wearing all black, white-faced Klaus Nomi doesn't normally sing behind rock stars. On his own, Nomi does this odd mix of opera and cabaret, and James is obsessed.

I wait until the show is done. Then ask, So you don't want to…I mean, you don't sing opera.

Oh, lord, no, James says. I just want to be that brave.

Brave?

James stares at the screen, which is still glowing bright, even though the set is turned off. Yes, he says. To be myself.

I glance at James. At his black-and-white striped T-shirt. Red bandanna around his neck. White vinyl boots laced up to his knees over black parachute pants.

And pretend I understand.

HEADLESS BODY IN TOPLESS BAR screams the *Post*'s headline.

Honestly. You can't make this shit up.

Becky sometimes makes her own clothes on a sewing machine she found on the curb outside her building.

It's a little beat-up, but still works, and lately she's been making increasingly odd headbands with things glued on top. Today, she's wearing one that has a tiger with a key around its neck.

What's the key for? I say.

My mom's car, she answers.

I know better than to ask.

I dream about Gabriel. About being kissed. About what comes next.

Becky sits in front of me in Mr. Solomon's class and I pass her notes:

How do I know?

What if?

What does it feel like?

We're supposed to be writing down questions to ask a class visitor, a girl who volunteered on a kibbutz in Israel, a kind of communal living thing.

Becky stretches and drops a crumpled paper behind her head and onto my desk. It says: *If you want sex, don't fall in love. If you want love, don't sleep with him.*

Her answer feels wrong. Limited. Like, there have to be more than two options.

Wait, I write back, *What if I want both?*

She never answers, and then the bell rings and I'm too embarrassed to ask her out loud.

James is going to his parents' house in Connecticut for the weekend, so he's smoking twice as much as usual.

We sit on the fire escape of his apartment, watching the hookers cruise Ninth Avenue.

You *could* live in a better neighborhood, you know. I mean, not like you can't afford it. Wouldn't your mother freak if she saw this place?

James laughs. Forget my mother. My father would have me locked up.

James sets his cigarette down on the edge of the rail and leans forward, elbow to knee.

This is what I know about James's parents: His mother is British and rich and beautiful and distracted by her clubs and her foundations and her committees. James loves her, although he wishes he didn't. His father is a wildlife photographer for a big glossy magazine and spends his life on safari and in the bush and anywhere but at home. James says he doesn't love him, but sometimes wishes he did.

Wouldn't your dad be used to this kind of thing? I ask, pointing to the rusty railing and the broken windows, the shattered crack vials and burned-out cars, and the guys sleeping in the doorway across the street.

James picks up his cigarette and takes a long drag before flicking it over the rail and into a stagnant pool of water.

My dad only shoots things he thinks are beautiful, James says, as if his father used a gun rather than a camera. He'd hate this.

Coming down the hall back in our apartment, I stop to listen to Mom on the phone.

I know, Connor honey, she says. I know. I know. Don't cry.

I retreat to my room, not wanting to intrude. Not sure, even now, how to merge the cocky version of my brother with the one who still needs to cry on the phone to his mother.

Sunday night, I wake up to the smell of smoke curling through my window, which I'd opened so I could listen to the sounds of the rain merge with the drone of the city. I crawl over and stick my head out.

Are you trying to drown your sorrows? I ask James.

I think mine have flotation devices, he responds, and shakes water out of his long hair.

I pull my head back, and he climbs in after me, shivering.

So the weekend was that good? I ask.

James helps himself to the towel from the back of my door and a sweatshirt from my dresser.

My father was almost mauled by a bear, James says. He made the mistake of getting between it and its lunch.

But he's okay?

James strips—I forget how thin he is under the shoulder pads and the scarfs and the jewelry—and shrugs into the Clash shirt that Connor put aside for me at the store. London Calling. Pretend you're a rebel, he'd said, and I didn't bother to figure out what he meant.

James doesn't speak until he's lit another cigarette and opened the window again to blow the smoke out.

71

We wait while a symphony of sirens plays and then streams away into the night.

My father is fine. My father is always fine. Of course, he neglected to bring me the one photo I asked him for, but what else is new?

What was the photo?

Oh, he says, waving his free hand, naked without his rings. Something for the new show. But that isn't really the point. Honestly, I think he'd be way more interested in me if I were a hyena or mountain lion. If I were something carefree and feral.

After the rain stops and James warms up and leaves, I lie in bed and stare at the ceiling. At the tiny blue star I've glued in the corner.

And I wonder, is everyone a mass of insecurity? Even James?

Our career assessments come back, and Becky and I wait until we meet up with James after school to open the envelopes.

According to this, I should either become a stewardess or join the military, Becky says. What the heck is that about?

Did you say you love travel? I ask.

Well, there wasn't a box for "get me the hell out of here."

I stare at my report for a long time. Long enough that she grabs it out of my hands and starts laughing.

Human services? What the hell is that?

That, James says from behind the new edition of *Backstage*, means that Michael should consider a career in psychology. Or social work.

The pages rustle.

Or, he continues, just write a whole lot of songs that people conceive babies to.

I grab the tabloid from him.

Did you ever take one of these? I ask.

James runs a hand through his hair and stretches his head backward like a cat in the sun.

I want to change the world, he says, horrified. I want be true to myself. I have no wish to be in a box.

Don't worry about that, Becky smirks. There probably isn't even a box big enough to hold your jewelry collection.

It's easy to coast during the day. Wake up. Go to school. Come home. Do homework. Go to sleep. Get up and do it again.

At night, when I can't sleep, and the sirens don't want to quit, or when my dad is yelling and my mom is trying to calm him down without pissing him off more, I lie here like a bystander, watching anxieties parade through my head.

First in line: Gabriel. Is this what Connor felt for Tony? This rush and hum that takes over my whole body when I even think of him? Is this why my brother did the loudest, the most public thing he could think of for a relationship he knew probably wasn't going to last? Because he couldn't hide the enormity of it anymore? Because it was so unfair that he'd even have to try?

Next up is Becky and how she deserves to be happy, but never really gets there, with her mom being one more thing she needs to take care of, and Andy never being around for her. I hate that I don't know how to help her.

James says he wants to change the world and that's fine because he probably will. When has James ever failed at anything? Except there's something…off…with him these days. Some wall has surrounded him that I don't know how to scale.

And at the end, I'm left only with this: I don't know what I want to do with my life.

And that might be the most terrifying thing of all.

My brother wants a loan.

My father says he'd rather buy Connor a gun that he can use if he wants to keep shooting his mouth off.

My mother says he doesn't mean that.

My father says is doesn't matter whether he means it because they don't have money to lend, and even if they did, they wouldn't be loaning it to Connor.

My mother reminds him that Connor is his flesh and blood.

My father says something about the "fag part" not coming from *his* side of the family, and I stick my head out my bedroom window and replace the yelling with the sound of trucks and car horns and the music from the Italian place across the street. If this is all there is to being an adult: fighting and hating and working to pay the bills, I'm not sure I want any part of it.

PART

TWO

The music comes and the music goes.

Sitting in American history class, I'm brimming with notes, overflowing with melody, spilling lyrics onto my textbook about the Civil War.

At home, my guitar is silent. Talk to me, I beg. Talk to me.

When I complain to James, he says, That's how you know you're an artist, Michael; the muse takes you as her fickle lover.

He's so serious. So intense. So driven.

He's some sort of prodigy. Some sort of genius. So hot.

These are the things said by people who don't know James well.

But that doesn't mean they're wrong.

There are bigger clubs than The Echo. Clubs that are more popular. Clubs that draw the rich kids with their rich clothes and their rich drugs. There are clubs that are wilder and dirtier; clubs where broken glass is swept off the floors more nights than not. There are clubs for girls, and clubs for boys, and clubs for those at every point in between.

There are the clubs that Connor goes to: pills on tongues, sex in balconies with boys whose names you never need to know, the strange freedom that comes from anonymity and loss of control. Clubs I'm intrigued by, but can't work up the courage to even walk into.

And it's okay because I feel like myself in The Echo. I feel like I'm home.

I lean against the speaker. Bauhaus is droning out "Bela Lugosi's Dead," and I can feel the scream of the bats in the treble, the dripping of fangs in the bass.

The notes are loud enough to make my teeth ache, concentrated enough to make me feel drunk. I close my eyes and the room spins and my head spins and I give in and let it, and then I wonder if this is what hard drugs feel like and if Nancy Reagan will tell us to "Just Say No" to music because nothing this good could possibly be legal.

Gabriel's arms, sudden around my waist.

Gabriel's breath in my ear.

He fakes biting my neck as the singer repeats "Undead"

over and over. I turn my head, bare my skin. Open myself up. Finally understand why people write love songs. Lust songs. Whatever.

Run away with me, he whispers in my ear.

My stomach leaps. I know he can't mean it. We've only seen each other at the club. Haven't exchanged phone numbers or addresses. Had we gone to school together, I'd have known him for only a week instead of seeing him a few times stretched over a couple of months.

But a part of me is already packed and out the door.

Instead of running away, we dance.

Whatever else we have or don't have...

Whatever else we do when we aren't here...

Whatever else we dream about or want to escape from...

...this rhythm has infected us.

When the room is too crowded, too sticky, too smoky, when the music turns to bubblegum pop and the floor fills with girls in leg warmers and boys in Chinos, we maneuver to the wall. Sweaty, spent, and, for a minute, satisfied.

Gabriel shakes his damp hair and smiles at me. Time stops.

Becky made me memorize a list of things *she* thinks I need to find out about Gabriel before I let myself fall too hard for him. His favorite color. His favorite band. What he does when he isn't at the club. Whether he's actually looking for a boy-friend. Whether he wants to be monogamous.

But her questions aren't my questions, and all *I* need to know is this: When he smiles at me as if he recognizes some-thing within me that I've never said out loud; when my vision narrows so that the only thing I can see is him; when he makes me laugh and then my laughing makes *him* laugh…it's too late for the rest to matter.

How do you write a song? he asks me. How do you come up with the ideas?

I consider the hours I spend moving my fingers over the frets, listening for a tune somewhere inside me.

The time it takes to run to Manny's Music and buy new strings.

The balls of paper stacked in the garbage can when I'm trying to write a lyric.

And I shrug.

Gabriel tells me he likes to hang out in Washington Square Park on Sundays and watch the boys playing chess. He doesn't ask me to meet him, but also doesn't tell me not to.

When I ask their advice later, James says to go, that Gabriel wouldn't have shared the information unless he was testing to see if I'd show up.

Becky says to stay away. That sometimes wanting is better than having—whatever that means—and I'm starting to wonder if what works for her and Andy is really what will work for me.

And no way am I asking Connor.

I take the subway to West 4th and then get off and grab the uptown train, heading home without even leaving the station.

Not good to be too overeager, but I spend a whole week second-guessing myself, anyhow.

James says to ask Gabriel for his phone number. James says to give him mine.

James says that I'm driving him up the wall by looking at the clock and pacing through the days. I ask him what I'm going to do if Gabriel calls and my dad is the one to pick up the phone.

James chews his lip. What did Connor do? he asks.

I glare at him and say, Well, yeah, look how that turned out.

Becky is working her way through a pack of clove cigarettes. When I tell her she might think about cutting back, she says, I don't really smoke them. Sometimes I just light them like incense, and sometimes I just kind of suck on them for the flavor. I used to smoke them, but they made my gums bleed, and my mom was getting mad at me, so I stopped.

Now that Mom's using again, I don't really care what she thinks, she says. But I still don't really smoke them.

I never ask Connor about his phone call with my mother, and I don't ask why he'd need a loan because my brother is, I guess, entitled to some privacy. Instead, I catch him midbite at our

Wednesday dinner and ask, Did you ever think about just sitting down and telling Mom and Dad you were gay instead of being such a drama queen about it and pulling that stunt at graduation?

Are you high? he sputters.

I wish, but no.

Connor puts his burger back on his plate and takes a deep breath. Okay, he says. Just for shits and grins, let's walk through this. I could have called a family meeting, but Mom would have cried and Dad would have dragged me to my room and pulled out my suitcase and shoved all sorts of useless crap in it while telling me I was a waste of plasma. Then he would have thrown both me and the suitcase out the door and told me not to come back.

Isn't that what happened, anyhow? I ask.

Yeah, he says and shrugs. But at least this way, I had witnesses.

I met someone, I tell Connor, to see how the words feel in my mouth, to make it real.

Boy or girl, he asks, his face shoved into the menu as if he hasn't been reading it since he was thirteen.

His name is Gabriel, I say.

Connor explodes in a laugh. Like the angel? he asks. Like the one that blows...

Stop, I cut him off before he takes the joke to where I know he's going, because I don't think "trumpet" is what he has in mind, and Connor never did learn to keep his voice down in public.

84

Besides, I say, getting in my own jab, who are you to talk, dating someone named Destiny?

I'm thinking of taking driver's ed next semester, I tell my father.

My father says no before I even get the whole sentence out. Then he says, What? You wanna be a cab driver or something? Forget it, I'm not buying you a car.

I wasn't asking you to buy me a car, I protest.

Then why waste your time and my money by taking driving lessons?

Because I'd like to get a car *someday*.

Then *someday* you can learn to drive it.

I haven't visited the fear room in a while, and when I do, the paper has been changed. I'm never sure if the librarians throw it out or the school counselors lurk around until they see someone writing something truly awful and then drag the student into their offices.

I'm disappointed not to see anything from the person I was talking to before, so I decide to start the conversation this time.

I met someone, I write. *Someone I really like and...*

I leave it hanging on an ellipsis because I don't know what the "and" is.

...and I feel more alive when I'm with him than I ever have before?

...and I don't want to end up out on my own like my brother?

...and I'm afraid?

Look what I got? Becky dangles a key in front of me the next day while we're sitting in Mr. Solomon's class waiting for the sub to figure out how to work the overhead projector.

What is it? I ask.

It's for the bomb shelter.

Bomb shelter?

She explains that when our school was built in the fifties, a bomb shelter was put in and stocked with canned goods and supplies in the event of nuclear war.

So…do you know something I don't know? Are the Russians attacking?

Becky smiles. No, I'm writing about the shelter for the *Spirit*. But the key also opens the door to the roof.

Oh?

Oh.

We hang out in the school newspaper office and wait until after the last bell. Then we walk through the theater and climb up a ladder onto the catwalk where Becky uses her key to open a door in the ceiling.

We stand on the tarred roof. From here, you can see Central Park. The Hudson. Lincoln Center.

Becks, this is…

Yeah.

We dangle our feet off the edge. Lie back and stare at the clouds.

My mom hasn't been home in two days, she says.

Oh, Becks…

The worst part is I'm not sure I care. I mean, of course I do, but I don't think I can save her. And I have to focus on school or I'm going to end up trapped like she is.

I reach for her hand and ask, Is there anything I can do?

Take care of James, she says. He seems off these days.

James?

I'm worried about him. Andy's mom was telling me stories about the patients coming into St. Vincent's and… Oh, Michael. I'm worried about him and worried about this plague and his theater friends, and I'm worried he's going to meet someone who doesn't even know they're sick and… I wish the two of you were together.

I take a deep breath. Then another. I get that she's worried about James, but her flood of words feels bigger than that somehow.

Is Andy's mom okay? I ask. Is she…scared?

Becky sits up and says, Of course she's scared, but she's volunteering to work in those wards; some of the nurses won't even go into them. I don't know what she's saying to Andy, but she keeps telling me not to assume that being a girl is going to keep me safe.

We're quiet for a long time after that until Becky shades her eyes and stares down at me. She says, I lit a candle for James in church last night.

Becks, about this whole church thing, I start as I sit up.

She grabs my hand again. You have your music, she says. Your dancing. Even your brother. Andy is always busy these days, I spend more time talking to his mom than to him. *My* mom is falling apart. I'm not sure how much I have. At least let me have God.

I squeeze her hand and stay silent. Even I'm not stupid enough to argue with God.

On Friday, I'm back at the club. Dancing with Gabriel. Losing myself in his eyes.

From the DJ booth Danni plays The Cure's "Let's Go to Bed." I'd forgotten how sad the lyrics of this song were. Lost love and misplaced lust. But it's still damn good to dance to.

I love the song enough to try to ignore the implications. Ignore the heat, and the need, and the invitation that's sitting on my lips.

Because we can't just go to bed, or anyplace else, really. *My* bed is in my parents' house. A fortress of hate.

But there's a pressure that's building, building, building. And Gabriel dances in front of me, white shirt pulling tight over his biceps, 501s hugging his ass, sweat curling his hair right above his collar.

Next is Berlin's "Sex (I'm A…)" and it's too much. I cough an apology to Gabriel and head back to the DJ booth. Danni pretends I'm not there.

Can you dial it back? I yell over Terri Nunn's percussive orgasmic notes.

Danni takes off his headphones. Don't know what you mean, Michael. I'm just playing what's making them dance.

I give up and get a Coke. Watch Gabriel watching me while I try to ignore the music, which is impossible when it's blasting loud enough to shake the walls. When it's making the hair on the back of my neck stand up. When it's echoing this hunger inside of me.

Gabriel makes a circuit from the dance floor to the bar where he borrows a pen and a napkin, writes a note, and brings to me.

Let's go somewhere more private is scrawled in swirling script.

It's like he's reading my mind. Giving me what I want. What I've wanted for a while. I hope he knows someplace.

But if it's what I want, why the hell am I so scared?

We stop just outside the door. Deafened by the sudden silence. Both aware that we've crossed the threshold from private to public. Outside, there's no bar or bathrooms or DJs or music. No crowd to lose ourselves in, no pillars to hide behind.

Outside The Echo it's only us, and the pressure to be in the real world, who I am at the club, is almost unbearable.

Where should we go? Gabriel asks too loudly because we've been screaming over the music for hours.

I mean, he asks—quietly now, smiling—Where to?

I shrug.

I've lived in the city all my life.

Connor and I learned to ride bikes in Riverside Park.

Our parents took us to Yankee Stadium before either of us could lift a bat.

I once walked across the Brooklyn Bridge with my eyes closed on a dare from Becky.

But I'm totally out of ideas for private places in New York City where two boys can go to make out.

On a whim, we take the L crosstown to the 1. We stand on the subway, shoulder-to-shoulder, barely speaking, hanging onto the same center poll, the vibrations from the tracks pushing us together, bouncing us apart, over and over.

Becky would tell me to make sure that someone knew where we were going, "just in case."

In case, I guess, Gabriel turns out to be a serial killer. Or in case the subway loses power, and we're stuck between stations, and my parents start freaking out. Or in case... Well, who knows?

It isn't that I disagree with her, but I'm so damned tired of doing the right thing all the time. Tired of being safe simply for lack of anything else to be.

In the garish light of the subway, against the thick black graffiti, and the advertising, and the dirt, Gabriel's smile is somehow even more intoxicating than in the club. And when he reaches over to fix my collar, his fingers linger on my skin, and that's intoxicating too.

I'm out of words, anyhow.

We get off the train at Christopher and walk through Sheridan Square, and then around a corner. It started to rain while we were underground, and the street is oddly quiet and dark under these huge un-city-like trees.

I don't spend a lot of time in the West Village, except when I visit Connor at work.

The gay stores, the gay boys, the gay girls, so sure of themselves and who they are, make me feel self-conscious. It isn't like I would change anything. And it isn't like I'm really in the closet. But it isn't as if I'm all the way out either; it's more like I'm standing in the doorway.

I don't walk around school advertising the fact I'm attracted to boys, and it's clear my parents sure as hell have no clue since they haven't kicked me out. I mean, Becky and James know, and Connor, and probably everyone at The Echo and maybe the staff of The Strand, if they bothered to look at the books I've read in their darkened corners.

And Gabriel. Gabriel knows, and Gabriel likes it.

He takes a step toward me and kisses me hard, like he needs to more than he wants to. I'm a mass of contradictions. Of live wires, electricity, and conga drums. Of caffeine and cotton candy.

His hand slips up the side of my shirt, and my muscles spasm against his fingers. The sky spins like I'm going to pass out, the brick wall of the townhouse the only thing holding me up.

This is different from being in the club. This is different from anything.

There was a boy in music class my last year at St. Sebastian's. His name was Eli, and he had a light Afro that he was forever combing with a pick. His skin was so smooth that I used to stare, wanting to reach out and touch it, and his voice was so soft I always found myself leaning toward him to listen. We stayed after school one day to help decorate the gym for the band concert and found ourselves standing behind stage when the lights suddenly cut. The only way out was on the other side of the room. We couldn't see a thing.

He took my hand and started to walk, but it felt like something more than two boys guiding each other through the dark.

91

Or maybe it was exactly that. Maybe we saw something in each other that we each needed to see, and we were trying to help each other.

We both hesitated before pushing the door open. In the darkness, I was aware of him leaning in toward me, close enough to feel his heat, drawing me in.

And then the power came back on.

Eli's family moved, and he transferred out a week later.

I always wondered what it would have been like to kiss him.

But I know now that it wouldn't have been like this. Gabriel tastes like cinnamon, and kisses me in a way I feel with my whole body. In a way that pushes reset on my world.

Some guy walks by and grunts "fags" under his breath, but I don't care. I'm falling, falling, falling. Feeling like I'm part of this city. Feeling like I'm part of myself. Feeling like being with Gabriel at this specific moment in time is my reason for being born.

Feeling like there's no damn reason for the whole world not to see us.

When we stop kissing and catch our breath, when the rain stops and we walk around, when shift change comes and yellow cabs flood the street, Gabriel says, My papa drove a cab. He was the best. He was always working. But he never missed a single one of my gymnastic meets. He sat in the front and yelled so loud he embarrassed me. I used to tell him, Stop, Papa. Can't you just clap like everyone else's parents? But I didn't really mean it. The first time I tried to compete after he died, I fell off the high bar. No matter what I did, I couldn't hold my grip. It wasn't important anymore.

We stop and listen to three girls sing in harmony for a while, and then I ask, Did he know? Did your father care that you were gay?

Gabriel looks off into the distance and then shrugs. I was doing a shitty job of pretending I was seeing Gloria then, he says with a crack in his voice that stabs me in the stomach. But my papa would have been cool so long as I was happy, I think.

I try to imagine what it would be like if my parents were "cool" and cared about me being happy. I wonder what it would be like to bring a boy home for dinner. For Connor to do the same. To be able to really talk to my parents. To be able to live without hiding.

I tell Gabriel about Connor being kicked out and then feel oddly guilty. My father wasn't always like this, I say to Gabriel. I mean, maybe he was, and it didn't matter because we were little and hadn't done anything to upset him. But I remember him teaching me to play catch and helping me with math homework.

Now I try to avoid him. I wish, I start to say…

What?

Nothing, I reply. True as it is, I can't bring myself to say the words or stop myself from wishing that his father were still around and mine were gone.

After it stopped raining, after we stopped kissing, after we stopped talking, Gabriel bought a pretzel from a vendor in Washington Square Park and held it out to me.

We break the dough like a wishbone. He gets the bigger piece and smiles mysteriously when I ask what he's wishing for.

We divvy up the rest of the pretzel and watch some guys dive off the side of the fountain into cartwheels and handstands.

Gabriel studies them and shakes his head. Their form is all off, he says.

Can you do better? I ask and swallow down a wave of excitement at the thought of him balancing and performing in front of me.

I'm rusty, he says. But I can see a hungry light in his eyes that kind of turns me on, and before I know it, he's pulling off his jacket and stretching out the muscles in his shoulders.

He says something in Spanish to the boys on the fountain, and they stop and slap his hand and give him room.

Then he's in flight. A blur of muscle and skin tumbling over the concrete so fast I don't think he's touching down.

He stops when the boys begin to applaud and comes back to me, barely having broken a sweat, rubbing his calloused hands on his jeans.

That was… I start to say. The rest of the words catch in my throat.

Told you I was rusty, he says. I haven't done that in a long time and concrete… My coach would have benched me for doing something so stupid.

I stare at him. His eyes are on fire reflecting the streetlamps, and there's a breeze that's ruffling his hair, and I'm acutely aware that no song I've ever written or even played is as intense as what I've just seen.

I'm still speechless as he pulls out his wallet and shows me a picture of himself with a little girl on his lap. She has dark pigtails and a huge smile, and she's looking at him with the same expression I probably have on my face, like I'm looking at someone so good he probably can't be real.

He says, That's Sophia, my little sister. She's why I gave it up. She's the reason I work so hard.

I cough to clear my throat and bring my thoughts back down to earth. You didn't want to finish school first?

After my father was killed, it wasn't about what I wanted. It was about not getting evicted.

Maybe you can go back someday, I say.

Gabriel turns and takes my hand, blocking the action from the boys with his body. His eyes are on his own rough hands as they run over my fingers, calloused from playing guitar.

Does it matter to you? he asks, not looking up. That I didn't finish school. Do you care?

What? No, I say, backtracking, because really, it doesn't make any difference. Then I add, But I'd like to see you do *that* again. I gesture at the fountain. You're really good.

He pauses. Then says softly, *That* was another life, but I'm glad you think so.

When he turns, opening us up so everyone can see, he doesn't let go of my hand.

I don't have your phone number, I joke as we get back to the subway station…well, half joke. How do I know you're really who you say you are?

Gabriel, serious, says, I'm never home. I'm like my papa, always working. I try to pick up odd jobs when I can. My mother cleans apartments all day while my sister is in school. At night, she needs to sleep so we keep the ringer off. Also, her English isn't so hot.

I nod like I'm okay with all of his justifications that sound to me like excuses. But I still wonder.

I miss my curfew.

Mom tuts. Disappointed. I thought we could trust you, Michael.

My father glares, face reddening as if he's been waiting for this moment since I was born. Where were you? he snarls. I hope to hell you have a good explanation.

I don't remind him that I'm only forty-five minutes late. Not like Connor when he used to stumble in at five in the morning, drunk and high and smelling of sex.

Still, I let my hand snake around my stomach, thinking of how Gabriel's was there a little over an hour ago.

The subway was late, I say, trying to keep my voice from shaking, not from fear but from an intense stab of desire, And the pay phone on the platform was broken, smashed to bits. You should have seen it.

I look straight at my father, daring him to come up with a response.

For a minute, I think he's going to hit me, although he hasn't gone there since I was ten. We stare at each other, and I realize we're the same height; I'm not sure when that happened.

He narrows his eyes and says, You're grounded for a week, and walks out of the room.

96

Mom?

Sorry, she sighs. You know how he is about breaking the rules.

Rules.

My father's rules:

→ *Don't make noise*
→ *Don't draw the wrong kind of attention to yourself*
→ *Don't stand up for anything you believe in*
→ *Don't show any emotion that isn't anger*
→ *Don't be yourself*

I'm working on that song for Gabriel. Trying to get the chords to fit together, only they're fighting me and each other. They're dissonant and ugly and not at all how I feel.

Except when I think about the fact that Gabriel won't give me his number, and then I'm all about the jarring notes.

What do you think of the space shuttle? Becky asks. I get to see her at school, which not even my father can forbid. The shuttle just landed, and like always, the teachers turn on the TVs, and all the classes cluster around, watching.

It's the first step toward jet packs, I say. Can you imagine that someday, this will be normal? Like, we won't even notice when shuttles are launching and landing. It will be business as usual and no one will care. Maybe we'll even colonize the moon or find life on Mars.

Maybe then everything on Earth will make more sense.

I duck into the library at lunch and head to the fear room, amazed that no one ever seems to use it the way it was intended.

Under my note about Gabriel, the one I couldn't finish is this: *And?*

I drum the pen on my palm.

I write: *I want to know everything about him.*

Then, I turn the period into a comma, and listening to a tiny voice inside me, I add, *but I think he has secrets.*

Becky says everyone has secrets.

I used to have this awful fear about having to choose which parent I wanted to live with if they broke up, she tells me. I always chose my mom, because she was fun when I was a kid and my dad was the one who made me do my homework. Then he left, and I felt like it was my fault.

After I hug her, I try to think of what secret I could share in return. Becky knows I'm gay. She knows I miss Connor, even when I'm giving him shit. The only thing she doesn't know is that I've always wished she were right about James being in love with me.

And I'm not telling anyone about that.

My parents are both out, so after school, Becky, James, and I sit in Connor's old room playing Pong. The TV is a little off-center, and you can't see one of the paddles, but I've gotten good enough that I can mostly guess where it is.

I'm two points up on Becky, when James says, So, where's Andy these days, kitten?

Becky drops the controller, and I score the winning point. Why? she asks. I can see her knuckles go white against the plastic knob.

James fiddles with an unlit cigarette. He doesn't look up when he says, Well, he's never around now, is he?

He's around enough, she replies, but her tone is defensive, and James and I both know he hit a nerve.

Before they leave, James grabs Becky's hand and spins her into his arms as if they're starring in some old MGM musical.

You know I only give you a hard time because I care, he tells her.

Do me a favor and care a little less, she says. In response, he smiles a smile that lights up the room, and I know that everything between them is okay again.

Saturday morning, I take a page out of my brother's book ("better to ask for forgiveness than permission") and leave the house before my dad is awake and complaining. I meet Becky and James outside The Strand. James has his head stuck in a book of Frank O'Hara poetry, and he keeps stopping to read bits of it to us as we walk through the Village.

Becky and I glance in the windows. Pastry shops. A cigar shop where Becky goes in and buys a pack of clove cigarettes. I took the money from my mother's purse, she says. I figured if she could buy drugs for her boyfriends, she could buy me a pack of cloves.

James pulls his head out of his book to respond, but I shoot him the same look I give Connor when I want him to stay quiet.

We pass a couple of sex shops. James keeps walking. I pretend to look away, glancing out of the corner of my eye. Becky stops in front of the window. Cocks her head. I wonder how you'd use that, she muses.

James and I keep walking forward, and she has to jog to catch up with us.

Later, James asks if we should be worried about Becky.

I don't know, I reply, but she said she's worried about you.

Why on earth would she be worried about me?

Before I can think better of it, I jump at the least frightening thing on Becky's list. She thinks you're lonely, I say.

He stops, leans back against the wall of a bodega, and takes a long drag on his cigarette. Why does she think that? he asks, measuring his words.

I shrug, regretting I'd said anything. You know her, I say. She thinks everyone should be in love.

James's eyes cloud over as they seem to do so often these days.

There's a reason that love is a four-letter word, he says as he pushes off the wall and starts walking again.

We're quiet until we make our way up the stairs to James's apartment.

She needs a name, James says, draping himself around an armless mannequin that one of the roommates found on the street. She's painted gold and wearing a shiny red ball gown with steel-tipped boots and a black scarf decorated with tiny white skulls.

You let my brother dress her? I ask.

James smirks, happy, I guess, to be speaking of things that don't matter. No, he says. But Connor gave me a ten-percent discount. Decent of him.

Mmmm... Well, don't let Becky see that dress. She'll be pissed you didn't loan it to her.

That's okay, James says with a glint in his eye. I have others.

There's a melody I can't get out of my head.

It might be the best thing I've written.

Now I'm worried I've heard it somewhere before.

From the radio? The club? Where have I heard it?

I hum it for Becky. For my mother. For James.

I play it in chords, major and minor.

What is it from? What is it from?

I call Connor and play it over the phone.

It's kind of like that stupid cat food commercial, he says.

Oh.

B-Side Records is hiring.

My parents have a thing against my working during the school year.

Also, if you listen to my dad, Connor met Tony at his part-time job at Canal Street Jeans, ergo working downtown can make you gay.

Yeesh.

It's too late anyhow. The next time I go back, the position has been filled.

Michael, stop it, Becky says for the third time. You're drawing attention to yourself.

The theatergoers mill around on 44th outside the Little Theater, finishing cigarettes, unwrapping candy, sharing their thoughts on the show's first act. We're supposed to be trying to fit in, which I'm apparently failing at.

Story of my life.

I lean in close to her so no one will hear me. But what if we can't find seats? I ask. What if the ushers realize we don't have tickets and kick us out?

Becky shrugs. James says people second-act shows all the time. And it's a Tuesday. The theater won't be that full.

Yeah, but… I start, and Becky gives me a withering look. The whole idea of walking into a Broadway theater without a ticket, following the paying ticket-holders back from intermission, and grabbing an open seat, scares the heck out of me.

But James was sneaky and Xeroxed the first act of *Torch Song Trilogy* for us to read. We have to see the rest of the actual show if we want to know what happens next.

And I *have* to know what happens next.

I've never seen a play with a gay character, much less a funny one.

The lead character, Arnold, is a drag queen (which I'm not) and sexually experienced (which I'm not) and Jewish (which I'm not).

But when his mother admits that she would have aborted him had she known he'd turn out gay, I felt it as if I knew him.

After all, my father is no different.

I cancel my dinner with Connor and see the second two acts of the play again on Wednesday.

Where are you applying to college?

I haven't really…

Where are you applying?

I mean, it's only junior year…

You need to think of your future, Michael.

My future?

You don't want to end up like your brother, right?

Oh. Yeah.

It's pretty easy to tell we don't have a dress code at school by looking at the Sex Pistol wannabes with their safety pins and leopard print and mile-high hair.

But still Andy stands out in his red Guardian Angel's beret and T-shirt against the gray lockers and beige walls. Maybe it's because I know him. Maybe it's because he seems more on-edge since taking this gig. Maybe it's because I'm worried Becky isn't happy.

Or maybe I'm just listening to James too much. Hard to tell.

Patrol is going good, Andy tells me. And Dad is cool with it so long as I don't work in the neighborhood. He says he doesn't want me being targeted or anything. But I think he just doesn't want me patrolling on his beat. But it's not a problem. I'd rather deal with the tourists, anyhow. I mean, man, we gotta start taking some responsibility for keeping our city safe, right? Before it turns into a total shithole. Like, last night I saw this old woman mugged on a subway platform while the transit cop was asleep in the car on the train. I mean, that's not right.

What did you do? I ask.

Andy readjusts his cap and says, Radar, that's my patrol leader, he took a picture of the sleeping cop to mail to his sergeant.

No, I mean, what did you do about the woman?

Oh, we chased the guy down and held him till the other cops came. By the time we got back, the woman was gone.

MAY 1983

I head downtown, but on impulse, I get off the subway at Times Square.

There's a buzz here. A dark and sexy underground buzz highlighted by the groups of sailors cruising in groups, dress whites shining against the grime of the X-rated movie houses and hot dog carts. Prostitutes, tourists, people strung out in doorways, business people hailing taxi cabs with their squealing brakes and cigarette roof ads, and plumbing smoke from the subways.

My mother hates it here. Thinks it's dirty and crowded and loud.

And she's right.

But somewhere in this crush, this hum, the music of this noisy, gritty, frenetic city, somewhere is a place where I belong.

I get back on the subway and head to the new almost block-long Tower Records. Lust after all the new releases waiting right inside the door. Wonder if CDs are really going to be a thing. Stare at the poster announcing that U2 is playing the Palladium on May 11. Wonder how I can get a ticket and what I can tell my parents that will get them to allow me to go to a show on a Wednesday night.

As I'm standing there, a guy in a T-shirt that says HONOR THE DEAD, SUPPORT THE LIVING pushes a flyer into my hands.

I take a ridiculously long time to read the sparse instructions that amount to: *Come to the march and candlelight vigil on May 2 to demand more money for AIDS research.*

It's tomorrow, the guys says, Make sure you bring a candle.

Then I step back and look around.

Is he giving the flyers to every guy who walks by?

Does he know I'm gay?

Do I want him to?

I'm not even sure it matters. If I'm not sure my dad will let me go see U2 on a school night, he's never going to let me go to an AIDS march, regardless of what night it's held.

Besides, I don't think I'm the demonstrating type. And no way would I go alone.

I walk away without going into the store. I feel too guilty and weirded out to go shopping.

In the end, James pulls some strings and gets me a ticket to see U2, and my father gives in when I tell him they're a religious band.

Three thousand four hundred of my new best friends and I sweat in a converted movie theater on East 14th Street while Bono waves a white flag and sings his heart out, stopping only during "I Will Follow" when people in the front threaten to get crushed.

The Edge and Adam Clayton swap instruments, and I'm surprised to find myself crying as the whole place sings along to their closing hymn "40."

Maybe what I told my father wasn't far off from the truth, I just wish church made me feel this high, as if I were made of music and community and goodwill.

Aside from brief phone conversations, I barely connect with James.

I leave messages for him. Becky leaves messages. When he wakes up, we're already in school. When we're home, he's already out at rehearsals.

He comes all the way uptown in the middle of the night to leave things taped to the outside of the metal mailboxes in our building's lobby.

Books. Cassettes. Tiny origami shapes: dragons and roses and stars.

My father sneers at these gifts when I don't get to them first.

My mother smiles sweetly as if they were meant for her.

Becky smirks at me and says, You don't see him coming to Queens to leave *me* presents, do you?

Well, it *is* Queens, I joke. But really, I know James isn't leaving me gifts as any sort of subtext. I've seen this before. He's restless with a type of endless creativity that forces him to keep moving until he can sleep.

It's this show, he says when I ask him. I might be in over my head this time.

You say that with every show, I remind him.

He brushes his hair out of his eyes, and I can see the results of his schedule. The dark circles under his light eyes, the chipped polish on his nails.

He says, This one is…never mind. I'm sure it will all work out.

You need a break, I tell him. But I suspect he needs more than that.

You think?

Yeah. Come out with me.

I can't just…

Yes, you can.

It's Friday night and I'm trying to play, but the strings on my guitar slip away from my fingers as if they're greased, and I have to admit to myself that I'm nervous. Not because James is coming with me to Echo. Not because I hope Gabriel is going to be there. Just something in that combination feels like acid in my stomach.

Maybe it's that James can be so damned charming, and it's

probably only a matter of time before Gabriel gets sucked into his orbit.

Maybe it's this feeling that there is so much Gabriel isn't saying. So much more I want to know.

Maybe I'm fooling myself about Gabriel's interest in me, and James will see right through it.

Maybe reality can never be as good as what's in my head, anyhow.

I think of telling James my mom won't let me go.

But then I picture Gabriel at the club, assuming that I'm pissed at him, damp bangs hanging seductively over his eyes, and Simon, a priest over at St. Bartholomew's—only none of us are supposed to know it—coming over and using his magnetic church voice on him. I'm a good listener, Simon always says. But from what I've heard, listening isn't the only thing he's good at.

Gabriel is Simon's type too, with his coal eyes and his easy smile and... I shake my head.

Let's get going, I say to James. I don't want to be late.

Danni waves as we walk in.

Brian pours me a Coke with extra ice.

James takes his place against the wall.

I wait.

The rituals of a night out.

Gabriel doesn't lean in when he talks to James. He stands right behind me. Close enough that I can feel the heat off his skin.

We're working up a show at The Space, James tells Gabriel in a way that makes it sound like the most boring thing in the world. It's a performance art piece about the cost of silence.

I've heard this speech before. So while James talks about the impossibility of ever achieving perfect quiet, given the body's tendency to beat and pump and gurgle, and the price of hiding yourself behind a public face and assuming your voice doesn't matter, I take a small step to the left and watch.

Gabriel stands straight. Tall. He links his thumbs in his belt loops, angles his head, allows his eyes to stray to mine. Making sure I'm watching him, which, of course, I am.

James speaks so softly that Gabriel has to take a step closer to hear him. James is exhausted, so maybe that's the cause of his quiet speech. It could be. But I don't think it is. He's too deliberate. Too aware. He leans an arm around my shoulder, trying to act casual, and pulls me close.

My arm moves around his back out of habit, and then I drop it when I see the questioning look in Gabriel's eyes.

And James. Here's the thing. When he looks at you, his attention can make the room a warmer place, but if he doesn't like you or isn't sure, those same eyes can make you turn away from their chill.

Gabriel is fighting it. Fighting him.

But I can't.

I pull away and wander to the bar. Gabriel's eyes heavy on my back.

Here, Brian places a Coke on the bar. Looks at me. Takes

the glass back. Adds a shot of something. You look like you need it, he says.

By the time I've finished sucking the drink down, my knuckles are white on the side of the glass.

Angry. Why am I so angry?

I turn back to watch Gabriel smiling, uncertain. And James. There's a standoff going on between them I'm not sure I understand.

I face the bar. Give me another, I say to Brian. He hesitates, but fills a glass and hands it to me.

This one goes down faster, and my head spins.

I glance back as Gabriel heads toward the bathroom. I head toward James.

That looked heated, I say.

James fiddles with a cigarette. Lights it. Blows out long and slow. Asks, Did it?

Eyebrow raised, he stares into the spinning lights. I recognize the pose. The posing. It's what the others get. The ones who aren't his friends.

I have to leave, he says in measured words. But you stay and have a good time.

Outside, my feet crunch broken bottles. Car horns wail. A cat in heat yowls. James's heels clack in front of me like a metronome.

I catch up to him and grab his jacket. Spin him.

What the hell is going on? I ask.

He opens his mouth. Closes it. The mask drips off his face. His shoulders slump.

I'm sorry, he says. I don't know what's wrong with me. Gabriel seems nice. You should be happy.

Some last bit of alcohol reaches my brain, and I have to lean against the wall. I struggle to wrestle James's words into sense.

But? I ask.

James fumbles in his jacket for another cigarette. Puts it in his mouth without lighting it. Takes it out again. Nothing, he says. Really, Michael. I'm down, that's all.

I see in his eyes how he's on the edge of falling into the kind of funk that envelopes him like a shroud from time to time. And I watch his eyes dart from the wall to the street, to the rust-stained car with the NO RADIO, ALREADY STOLEN sign. Everywhere but at me.

He says, It isn't you. I'm just...

He waves his hands. Lost, he says. I don't know where I'm going.

The light on the corner changes to red. It reflects off James's pouty lips and stupidly, I'm drawn in. Desperate and helpless, I do what I've never had the guts to do sober, I kiss him. Quick. One kiss to stop the hemorrhaging.

James freezes. Pales. Takes a step back.

Oh, shit, I say. Sorry. Sorry. Sorry. The whiskey threatens to come out with my words.

No, Michael, he says, eyes still wide. You don't understand. This has nothing to do with you. I just can't...

His words trail off and we stand there, soundless for an unmeasurable amount of time.

I think of the boys. The girls. All the beautiful talented people who want to circle in his orbit. I know I'm no match for them.

That was stupid of me, I say, hoping the alcohol will numb the pain of his answer.

Oh, Michael, he says softly. I adore you, but…

His eyes are sad and the "but" hangs in the air. I prepare myself for the end of our friendship.

Sorry, I say, and turn to leave, Never mind.

Michael, James calls out, stopping me where I stand. You read that article. And Steven's sick, and I just don't. Anymore. I…can't.

I turn back.

Tiny pieces of James's life away from Becky and I jam into place.

You and Steven? I ask, my heart suddenly beating too hard. Holy shit, you aren't…

James leans back against the side of a phone booth and tries to smile. *That smile.* Ironic. And now I can see that this smile is something he keeps in his pocket and pulls out for effect.

No, he says, grin fading. No, we're not. We didn't. But there *was* one night. A party. We were interrupted. The power went out, and Rob needed to get into my room to reset the breaker.

I'm sure there's a metaphor somewhere in there, he says, offering me an attempt at a joke.

I exhale, relieved when I didn't even know that I should have been worried. James is okay. Of course he is.

But before I can question him more, he says, I'm not as brave as you think. Not anymore, Michael. Not at all. To come so close…

And then he shakes his head and walks away.

113

Hungover.

My dad blares the Yankees, swearing when Winfield strikes out.

I roll over, but my stomach stays still. Start to sit up. Lick my lips.

Remember my stupidity.

James's response.

His secrets.

The shift of reality.

Leaving without going back to the club.

The taste of guilt on my lips.

I sit in bed, homework looming.

I should call James. I should call Connor. Maybe Becky can tell me what to do. How to feel.

Then my mother yells down the hall that James is here, and I'm sure he's come to end our friendship. I have no idea what I was thinking when I kissed him. No idea what I've changed. If you move one grain of sand, then the world will never be the same.

Crap. That sounds like James.

But no. He comes into my room where he's spent so much time, only now it feels awkward, both of us unsettled.

He tells me that after I left, he went back to the club. Back to talk to Gabriel. Apologized.

He hands me a folded slip of paper. Seven digits.

The holy grail of Gabriel's pager number.

Call him, James says. He thinks he upset you.

The paper is hot in my hand. *Of course* Gabriel would give it to James. No one ever denies him anything.

I'm sorry, I say again.

I'm not sure what I feel worse about. My impulsive and ridiculous kiss? For not sensing that my best friend is going through stuff I know nothing about?

Or maybe for not even considering that something as ugly as this plague could ever touch James who is young and healthy and beautiful?

He shakes his head from side to side, and his bangs fall into his face. He pushes them back. It's okay, he says, looking relieved to have shared some of his secrets. You had no way of knowing. I should have told you, but it isn't something you can simply bring up in casual conversation.

And no one since Steven? I ask. What about all of those people onstage?

Not for real, no. Theater is different, he says. That isn't me.

For the first time ever, I feel sorry for James.

Sorry that he's turning his back on everything I want.

Sorry that he's afraid.

Sorry that I don't think I want to live my life in fear.

After James leaves, I call Gabriel and leave a message on his service, wondering why someone who has to work delivering balloons even has a service. Or a pager.

Then I wait.

And wait.
And wait.

He calls me back long after I'd given up hope, long after I stopped pacing in front of the phone and looking side-eyed at my mother when she said she needed to call the dry cleaners to see when my father's suits would be ready. He calls when I'm in my room hunkered under the covers, Connor's hand-me-down Walkman playing Joy Division on repeat, telling myself that Gabriel isn't going to call and I need to get over it.

I was thinking about you, he says.
Why?
I was thinking about when I was kissing you on Christopher Street.
Oh.
I was thinking that I wanted to do it again.
Oh.

The Islanders win their fourth straight Stanley Cup, but I don't care. It isn't that I don't like hockey, it's that their constant winning has gotten kind of boring.
And it hard to care about things like sports at the moment.

James has been busy. Always out. Always working.

He's sleeping during the day, rehearsing and plotting lights and weighing in on costumes and lines and meanings, all night.

At least that's what he tells me.

I finally reach him and ask if I can come over to watch *20/20* since Geraldo Rivera is doing a report on a friend of a friend of his, a lighting designer with AIDS. It's the first network report on the disease, and there is no way I'm going to get away with turning it on at home. My father would probably throw the set through the window, worried that he could catch something through the screen.

I'm not watching it, James says when I ask him. I just can't. But you're welcome to come over here anyhow; I'm sure the boys will have it on.

Which is what I do.

I sit on the couch (Steven's couch) with Rob, while Ted leans expressionless against the wall behind us.

No one is flirting tonight. We're barely breathing.

The guy being interviewed is twenty-seven. Eleven years older than me.

In his "before" photo, he's someone I might have found myself attracted to.

In his interview, he's dying.

Worse than dying, which I never thought could be possible.

Distorted. Marked with purple splotches. Terrifying.

I'll never be able to get his face out of my mind.

My father watches the 6:30 p.m. news. At 7:00 we eat dinner. That's the way it's always been and the way it always will be.

My mother drafts me into chopping vegetables. From the living room, my father shouts at the TV: They should be quarantined, all of them!

Stupidly, I ask what he's talking about. My mother sends me a warning glance. She's right. I should know better.

Queers, drug addicts, and Haitians, he yells back.

My knife stops midstrike.

Your sainted *New York Times* even said it, he yells to me. A researcher says you can get *it* from close contact with family. These deviants like your brother are going to kill us all. You watch.

When I tell James about the news piece, he nods. I know we're young, he says. But how do you fool around with someone while you're wondering if letting your guard down could get you sick?

The sainted *New York Times*, he continues, which is, I think, what I'll call it from now on, just wrote that the AIDS mortality rate is forty percent and getting worse with four new cases per day.

I understand James's fear in my head. How do you argue with something like that? But it's hard to think that I'm really at risk. I haven't had sex, and I don't do drugs, and I can barely find Haiti on a map.

But who really knows what will happen in the future, right? I mean, that's the problem isn't it? No one knows.

I love my music. I hate my music. I can't even listen to this crappy song. I should give up. But wait, that lyric is nice and

118

with the right backbeat it would work. Maybe I should record it and send it out?

Becky thinks her mom is using hardcore again. Or maybe the new guy she's seeing is. Becky isn't sure, but she found a used needle in the bathroom and Becky is determined not to go through *that* again, the endless cycle of dragging her mom home from bars and riding her bike around at night, checking alleys.

It's not like I'm asking her to stay home and bake cookies, she says, but can't she find a guy who *only* likes to drink?

It's my father's birthday.

As far back as I can remember, we've celebrated our family's events at Mama Patsy's in the theater district. At first it was some combination of my parents, me and Connor, and my aunt Bettina before she moved to Florida, plus my grandparents before they died.

I kind of thought we'd skip it this time. Given that it will probably be just me and my parents, I'd hoped we would.

But no, my mother reminds me. This is tradition. Family.

As if that really matters anymore.

Is Connor coming? I ask.

Mom looks away, a sure sign she's lying, since she knows she has no poker face. She says, He told me he might have to work.

Bullshit, I say, before I can stop myself. So much for tradition.

I head to the phone in the kitchen, ignoring my mother's admonishments to watch my language.

Please don't leave me alone with them tonight, I say as soon as my brother picks up the phone.

He sighs, then asks, And what exactly am I supposed to say over the rum cake? Happy birthday, Dad. Thanks for kicking me out and telling me I'm everything wrong with the world today.

Whether I want to admit it or not, my brother has a point.

He won't make a scene in public, I say, which is true. Even when Connor pulled his stunt at graduation, my father stayed quiet until we got home. Then there was nothing quiet about him as he started yelling and throwing Connor's stuff out of the apartment.

Why don't you bail? Connor suggests. We'll meet up with some of my friends. We can dance and pretend we're orphans. It'll be great.

I pull the phone away from my ear and stare at the receiver. I want to hang with my brother, but I must be more like my mom than I want to admit, because I don't know how to do anything aside from keep up appearances. I'm not ready for the fight.

Have fun for both of us, I mumble to my brother and hang up.

According to the menu, the restaurant opened in 1906, and obviously hasn't been updated since.

Also, I'm pretty sure the members of the waitstaff are all originals as well. Old Italian men in stiff black suits and ties.

Only tonight, our waiter is young. Not only young, but attractive with smoldering dark eyes and curly dark hair.

His name, according to his tag, is Pietro, and I can't keep

my eyes off him as he pours water for my parents and drops rolls on our plates with silver tongs.

I busy myself by folding and refolding my napkin, but then it falls to the floor and Pietro is there to pick it up and, with one deft move that makes my breath stick in my throat, sweeps it back onto my lap.

Probably a good thing Connor isn't here. I can't imagine my brother keeping his hands on his puttanesca.

Frank Sinatra plays in the background, and I listen to him sing about loving someone all the way while my parents talk about some movie they've seen, and about my mom's second cousin who is about to have her gallbladder taken out, and about Reggie Jackson striking out two thousand times.

My whole goal for the evening is to keep things on an even keel. I manage to stay quiet. Twirling my linguini, rolling cherry tomatoes around on my salad plate, staring at Pietro, sipping my Coke until the talk turns to this article in the *Post* by some commentator who says that AIDS is nature's way of declaring war on homosexuals who have declared war on it. I hear the familiar rise in my father's voice. Then I blurt out, "I think I'm flunking chemistry," which isn't true, but is better than where this conversation is headed.

I have to backpedal on the flunking thing when my father starts talking about more time spent on homework and less time spent with my friends.

But at least I circumvented another conversation about people deserving to die. '

The Spirit publishes a pro/con editorial about the Guardian Angels.

On the pro side is that they're keeping the streets safer just by being seen. They don't even have to take action most of the time.

On the con side is the potential for things to get out of control. For the Angels to overstep their rights and piss off the police. For people to get hurt by a group of civilians trying to enforce laws they may not understand.

Neither article is bylined, and Becky avoids my stare when she hands the copies out in class. But later I see her smile cryptically when some kids are debating the issue in the hall.

After school, Becky and I meet to work on our final project for Mr. Solomon's class on the meaning of happiness. Which really means we're hanging out in my room with James, talking about it.

We already read about things that affect quality of life like money, marital status, and friendship. Then we created a form asking kids in the class about people they know who seem happy. Asking them to list the things that make *them* happy.

It ends with this question: I feel most happy when (<u>fill in the blank</u>).

I feel most happy when everyone gets out of my way, says Becky.

What about you? I ask James.

He thinks while he rubs the nap of his black velvet pants in the wrong direction, leaving dark lines in the fabric. I'm happy when I'm creating something that wasn't there before. When I'm changing the world for the better, even in a small way, he answers finally.

What about you? he asks me.

I think and think, long enough that Becky has to flip over Bowie's latest LP and still I can't come up with an answer.

Somehow the conversation turns to Gabriel.

It's not fair that we haven't met him yet, Becky says. After all, you've both known Andy for years.

Known would be pushing it, don't you think, kitten? James says in his best fake Cockney accent. He's putting it on. Even when he's drunk, which he's not, given that it's four in the afternoon and we're sitting in my room and not a bar, James's real hint of accent is pure posh London.

You can stop at any time, Becky says.

I'm only looking out for you, he answers.

If I were you, I'd…

Hey. Don't make me stop the car, I interrupt. I try to turn it into a joke. But really, I'm not sure I can handle them fighting. It's a gift that James is even here and trying to take some time off from the show.

I don't know what it means that neither of us told Becky about James coming with me to Echo.

And about what happened after.

About what he told me.

About his fear.

Maybe you should come to Echo with me next time, Becks, I say, flooded with guilt.

The words are out and I can't take them back.

Gabriel isn't at the club.

It feels like a different place without him now.

I dance with Becky, who is wearing an angled, belted, hot-pink jacket she got from Connor that makes her looks a bit like an alien and a ribbon on her head as big as a watermelon that she got from a dollar store in Queens that makes her look like a birthday present. Somehow she manages to make them look as if the two things belong together.

Danni plays Madonna's "Burning Up" for like, the thousandth time, and the air must be out because the club is so hot the mirrors in the bathroom are fogged up.

I stare at my watch, wondering if I said something wrong on the phone when Gabriel called. If I should have said more. If I wasn't interesting enough, effusive enough. If I was supposed to flirt. Was that it? Does he think I didn't like kissing him? Does he think I regret leaving him a message? Does he still think I'm mad at him? Did he say he'd be here this week or did I imagine that? Had I reacted differently, would Gabriel be here now? Would I want him to be here, talking to Becky about school and my parents and all that run-of-the-mill, daily life stuff?

Someone bumps into me, and I turn to see Vampire Boy. He stares at Becky, then at me, and smirks as if my rejection has anything to do with her.

You suck, I say to him. And then laugh at my own stupid joke.

Becky stops. Shocked, I think, at my uncharacteristic nastiness.

The boy looks at me, bares his pointy teeth, and smiles before he walks away.

I guess I can see why you like it here, Becky says. I mean, the boys are mostly cute, and the music's mostly good, and it's close to the subway, and I like that smoke machine they have, and the lights, and...

I let her talk, lost in my self-doubt, until she says, I don't understand why James likes it, though, and then waits for me to explain it to her.

Huh. Why not?

Well, it doesn't exactly give him a place to show off.

Well, really, he doesn't even dance when he comes with me, I explain.

Sounds like he's found a way to stand out, then. Just by doing the opposite of everyone else.

As usual, she has a point.

As usual, I'm not sure why it really matters.

Half an hour till curfew and I'm still at the all-night diner with Becky.

She says, If I can hold it together through senior year, I think I might move in with my dad's cousin in Michigan and go to community college there. If I stay with my mom...

I let her words drop off and resist the urge to beg her not to leave. Sounds like a plan, I admit, but what about Andy?

She swirls her coffee cup, looking into it as if it will give her the answer to my question. She sighs and says, I figure I can't miss him any more than I do now.

I don't look at her when I ask, Have you thought of breaking up with him?

Sure, every time James suggests it. Not like I'm about to take relationship advice from him, though.

Why not?

Look. I love James, of course I do. Everyone loves James. But don't you think there's something a little bit… I mean, lately he can't even get himself sorted out.

I used to think James was one of the most "sorted-out" people I knew. Maybe he still is. Maybe he's the smart one, and everyone should hunker down and wait all this out.

I don't want to judge him for being scared. I wonder how Steven is and wonder what James isn't saying.

I wonder what it means for me when I'm so tired of waiting.

So, even though I'm hopped-up on caffeine and exhaustion, I find a way to keep my mouth shut. I'm sad that we're starting to keep secrets from each other and have to wonder what James and Becky are saying about me when I'm not there.

I tell Connor I want to meet him for coffee, because I haven't seen him for a while and dinner seems like too large of a commitment for him to make to me these days.

What are you going to owe me for this time? he asks, as if I can't just want to hang out with my older brother.

Nothing, I only…

You're the worst liar in the world, he says, but agrees to meet me at Astor Place, anyhow.

When I get there, Connor is spinning the Cube, a huge black sculpture that's really called *The Alamo*, for some unknown reason, as James has told me more than once. I stand on the corner and watch my brother, running in circles, a childlike smile on his face that I haven't seen in years.

On the other side of the Cube is a cute Black guy, his short hair dyed baby blue with that stuff they sell at Trash and Vaudeville. He keeps looking back over his shoulder at Connor, and now I understand my brother's smile.

I wonder if I'm interrupting something or if they've just met, because Connor seems to have the ability to meet people everywhere: on the subway platform, in the store, once he even hit on a guy who came into his sociology class to discuss what it was like having a brother who was a priest.

My brother is an equal opportunity charmer.

This is Greg.

My brother introduces us. Makes some pointless joke about my needing to use him as a cover for whatever evil thing I'm about to do.

We buy coffee from the bodega across the street. It comes in those same Greek diner cups that all coffee in New York City seems to come in. The side reads HAPPY TO SERVE YOU. The

127

design is called Anthora, according to James, although I have no clue what that means, and I really don't care so long as it keeps the coffee where it's meant to be.

So seriously, Connor asks, what are you up to?

Greg interrupts him, all Southern drawl and old-world charm. Cute boy like your brother, why wouldn't he have plans?

Then he winks at me.

I think of explaining to Connor that I've missed him and that I'm not sure how long I can or want to keep living a lie at home. I want to pick his brain for ideas, get his advice.

Then my brother gives me the once-over, leans in to Greg and says, Don't let him fool you. Michael's only plans are playing with himself and his guitar.

And that kills *that* idea.

There's an end-of-year school talent show and I consider entering, but then James reminds me that people with talent don't enter school talent shows, so I crumple up the entrance form instead.

I've memorized Gabriel's pager number, shoved the paper in my closet under a pile of sheet music, my old baseball cleats, a sweater.

But I haven't used it again.

And he hasn't used my number either.

He hasn't been to Echo for the last two Fridays, and I've developed a ritual. I have to hold my breath as I walk by the bodega and read the headlines of the *Post*. Only then will I avoid seeing something dire: an apartment fire, a hold-up, some random subway shooting like his dad. Only then can I believe I'll see him again.

I focus on writing music for James's show.

Try to teach myself to play dissonant chords, wrong notes, out of tune.

I drag out a metronome and try to play something that sounds like a drumbeat. A car crash. A lullaby.

Somehow, everything I play sounds like the same thing: longing.

JUNE 1983

Connor calls and cancels our dinner. He says, I can't get out of bed.

You don't have a key for the handcuffs?

Ha! No, really. I'm tired. I feel like crap. You think you can get Mom to make me some soup or something? he asks.

I think about it. Of course she'll do it. I might have been the one that Dad wanted to come with him to ball games and for brunch at church, but Mom loves nothing more than doting on her eldest son who always made her laugh and would watch endless old black-and-white movies with her.

I have nothing else to do, so I ask Mom to whip up some mushroom barley and offer to take it over.

Mom sighs wistfully as she ladles it into Tupperware containers. She says, Boys always need their mothers. Especially when they aren't well.

I choke on her sense of denial, wondering if she even believes what she's saying.

Still, as she continues to pour soup, I resist the urge to remind her that she did nothing when Connor *really* needed her to keep my father from kicking him out of the house. Maybe she tried, and Dad shot her down too. Maybe she's made the same pact with the devil that I have, and silence is her security blanket. Her safety net.

Connor is huddled on the couch under 142 blankets.

You really *do* look like crap, I say.

He pulls the blankets aside, and I see he's wearing mismatched pajamas. I didn't know he owned pajamas, and I'm not sure I've ever seen him in anything mismatched. There are dark circles under his eyes, and he winces whenever he swallows.

What happened to Destiny, anyhow? I ask.

You know, stairs, he croaks out. And, well…Greg.

Okay, so why isn't *Greg* here taking care of you?

It isn't that kind of thing, Connor says.

And your four thousand friends?

Connor sighs. I didn't want them to see me like this. No offense, but I don't really care what you think I look like at the moment.

I avoid offering a comeback only because his voice is weak, and I can still hear his raspy breathing as I step over to rummage around the small kitchen. I reach into a cabinet and pull out a stuffed Dalmatian, a saddle shoe with MAURICE printed across the bottom, a huge bag of weed.

Eventually, I find an empty pot in the oven, heat Mom's soup, and take it to him.

While he's sipping it out of a mug that says GAG ME WITH A SPOON, Connor says, I always thought I'd be the kind of big brother who could teach you stuff. You know, how to be a man and all that shit.

I stare at him. I can't even think of Connor as an adult, much less a man. And also, he must be feverish. This isn't the type of stuff my brother and I talk about.

Well, you know, I still have Dad, I say, and we both crack up.

I wash out my mom's Tupperware in the tiny kitchen sink, leave a stack of quarters on the table for laundry, and ask Connor, Do you think Dad kicked you out for being gay or for embarrassing him in public?

Connor blows on his soup and rakes a hand through his uncharacteristically unwashed hair. What? he asks, suddenly angry. You think you can finesse this? You think you can go home and tell him you're screwing some guy in a way that will make him pat you on the back and offer you a beer?

No, I answer, I just... I don't know.

Michael. He pauses and shakes his head. Don't be an idiot.

133

Music has always been my sanctuary. But now it's only a loud voice in my head.

When are you going to play a show, Michael? A gig? Music in front of real people instead of the dusty photos that sit on the bookcase?

John Lennon was sixteen when he formed the Beatles. Don't get me started on Michael Jackson either.

You're already past your prime.

We never go to Becky's, for obvious reasons. And James's place is crowded, so we're at mine. Dad is working late and my mom is helping with a bake sale at church. I keep hoping she'll see Father Simon for the lech that he is, but it's unlikely. She doesn't even know her own sons.

We're hanging in my room listening to records—Depeche Mode, Split Enz, R.E.M.—and building a giant house out of playing cards, which James keeps leaning in and blowing over before it can fall. Meanwhile, Michael Stipe is singing on my turntable, but I can't understand what he's saying, and the band refuses to print lyric sheets, a personal pet peeve of mine.

Do you have a CD player yet? Becky asks James.

The jury is still out on those things, he says as he replaces the ace of hearts. I mean, there's purity in hearing the music the way it was created, but there's also something to be said for the accumulated history of records. Those scratches and pops were earned.

Becky smirks. Sorry I asked, she says.

Then she reaches into her bag. Here, she says, I got this off the bathroom wall at The Echo.

She holds out a grimy scrap of paper.

I draw back and ask, You actually touched something in The Echo's bathroom and took it home with you? Why aren't you wearing gloves?

James leans over her shoulder. A phone number? I didn't think you were that hard up, kitten.

She elbows him in the ribs, but he laughs.

I think that's how Connor met his last boyfriend, I joke and then realize it's been a couple of days since I heard from him.

No, she explains. The sign said: *Dial-a-Daze: Call in times of questioning to be moved toward times of transcendence.* I'm curious, can we call?

Becky's eyes are lit up, and I shrug. Is it local? My parents will be pissed if they get hit with a charge for long distance.

Becky nods.

Sure, why not, I say. I haven't seen her excited about anything in a while.

She gets to the phone before I do, while James opens the kitchen window and lights up, trying not to catch my mother's pink gingham curtains on fire.

Becky waits until the sounds of sirens on the street fade away, and then she dials and holds the phone receiver out to us.

We lean in. There's a pause. Then a smoke-worn voice whispers, The world is made up of pieces. Scraps of paper. Broken concrete. Incomplete thoughts. We fill in what isn't there. Sew it together. Seep around each other's edges.

Becky lets the message repeat. Hangs up. Aside from James drawing on his cigarette, we're silent.

It's true, you know, James says after a while. It's the things

135

that are missing that keep us searching for a reason to stay alive.

Well, aren't *you* in a profound mood, Becky says.

Well, what do you think? James asks me.

My mind goes to Gabriel.

And strangely to my brother who always seems like he's looking for something he may not recognize when he finds it.

What I say is, I think this guy has too much time on his hands.

That doesn't keep Becky from wanting to call again at lunch the next day from the pay phone outside school.

Today, the voice simply says, Don't be the wound.

What the hell? she asks.

Maybe it means not to make things worse? I offer.

Or not to be the thing that hurts? she counters.

Yeah, but you can't blame something for hurting itself, right?

Obviously, she sighs, you haven't seen my mother lately.

The paper in the fear room is full. *I think I might have crabs* is written next to *I cheated on my French exam because I'm worried my grades aren't good enough for college and my parents will kill me if I don't get into their alma mater,* and *I'm not sure how I got home from Julie's party on Saturday night.*

I find a small square of open space and write about something that's been eating at me. *I got this flyer about an AIDS demonstration, but I was too afraid to go. And I kind of hate myself for that.*

136

I stop in after school, expecting my mysterious writer friend not to have answered yet, but instead, there is this: *No point in hating yourself. I've decided that living your life the way you want is the best revenge,* he writes. I'm assuming it's a guy. *I mean, otherwise you're letting those dicks win. And then what's the point of anything?*

I consider writing something about James. Or Gabriel. Or Connor who is still sick, and that fact scares me more than I'm letting on.

Instead, I write, *Is that what you do?*

Summer break is looming and B-Sides is hiring again. Something must be going on with my parents because this time, even *they* are warming up to the idea.

If you get a job, you can help with the groceries, my father says.

If you get a job, you might meet a nice girl, my mother says.

If you get a job, they won't know where to find you and you can stay out all night, Connor says.

If you get a job, maybe you'll be happier, Becky says.

If you get a job, you may never have time to write another song, says James.

I sometimes forget what being in school was like, James says.

I have a hard time picturing what real life will be like, I reply.

Really? James looks at me through his lashes. Who ever said anything about life is real?

Despite James's concerns, I fill out a job application at B-Sides.

Name. Address. Phone number.

Experience.

Um.

I write: *I've shopped here. A lot.*

Then I cross it out and write: *I'm a musician.*

Then I cross *that* out and replace it with: *I play guitar.*

But that isn't right either.

I'm not James. No one is writing about me in newspapers or buying tickets to hear me play.

Does it count if you make something that might possibly be called art, but no one hears it?

I cross out *I play guitar* and write *I love music*. No one can argue with that.

It's stifling hot as James and I walk through Central Park, even though we've waited until almost sundown to come out; all so he can check out Belvedere Castle for use as a future performance area. The castle isn't really a castle. James calls it a "folly," and it's more like multiple flights of stairs that ascend to a turret that has just reopened after a massive renovation.

As we approach, James surprises me by running up the stairs and sticking his head out of the window, shaking his hair like Rapunzel. I miss seeing him this way. Light and happy. It doesn't seem to happen much anymore.

He runs back to ground level and grabs a handful of what Connor and I call helicopter seeds, but which James says are actually called samaras, and takes them back to the top of the turret. Then he instructs me to stand underneath while he drops them down around me, the seeds swirling and spinning like dancers.

Is this helping you decide about whether to stage a show here? I call up to him.

He laughs. Starts to answer. Then stops. The shower of helicopters stops as well, and I look up to see what has him distracted.

You should come up here, he calls down soberly.

Seriously? There's like, a hundred steps in this thing.

Still, because it's James and because I'm curious, I haul myself up the stairs and look in the direction he's pointing. Hundreds and hundreds of people are making their way through the park carrying signs with numbers on them. A somber parade.

I don't get it, I say.

It's a memorial, James explains and then falls silent.

I squint and can barely make out the migration of people, some in wheelchairs, some leaning on arms, making their way across the park. Then I don't have to ask what the memorial is for. If we were trying to hide from this thing, we were fooling ourselves. It's going to keep going until it's found us.

What are the numbers on the signs? I ask, not expecting James to have an answer. My heart is suddenly beating too hard, and I can't blame the heat.

One for each of the dead, James says in a monotone. I forgot this was today.

We watch with a strange sense of sadness and fascination. Then James turns to face me, says, The guy on that *20/20* interview you saw, died four days after it aired. He's one of the people this is for. He wanted everyone in New York to know what's going on.

James shakes his hair out of his eyes. *You* need to know what's going on, Michael, he whispers, his voice nearly taken by the breeze, As much as they're telling us anyhow.

Then, weighed down by what we've seen, neither of us says anything else as we walk home, except to say goodbye at the subway.

Becky has nothing to do and Andy is on patrol, so I give in to her pleading to go see *War Games* at the Loews on 83rd.

Three-fifty for a movie ticket? Are they kidding? Becky grumbles as she digs out her money.

I'll pay you back, I say.

No, I invited you. It's really the principle of the thing, she says. They're going to play the movie whether the theater is full or empty, so why not cut people a break?

We get our tickets and popcorn, and grab two seats in the middle. I consider telling her I'm worried about Connor, and about the memorial James and I stumbled onto, and about what I know about why James is being so withdrawn, but then the movie starts, and it feels good to lose myself in something.

Even if that something *is* the idea that we're only a Galaga game away from nuclear war.

As we walk out after the movie, Becky grabs my hand and asks, You don't think that could really happen, do you?

I shake my head. The idea of someone using a game to get into government files sounds absurd. I tell her, James says it's ten grand to buy one of those new Apple computers for your house. Who the hell is going to fork out that kind of money?

Her hand relaxes in mine. You're right, she says, not like Russia is wired into the local video store.

I think about telling her that I have a feeling what we need to be afraid of is far, far closer to home, but I don't because I'd rather do the worrying for both of us.

Less than two weeks left of junior year.

I used to look forward to summer vacation.

Visits to our grandparents' place upstate.

Connor and I playing ball in the local league.

Camp.

Coney Island.

Free time.

Fun.

This year, Connor is working. Or not feeling great. Or both.

And neither of my parents have asked about my plans.

Have you seen this? Becky asks days later, slipping a page from the *Village Voice* into my hands during homeroom.

She leans over my shoulder and reads out loud: *The Club 99 Arts Group has cemented their next piece with the addition of wunderkind James Barrows, last seen in the group's production of Kurt Weill and Bertolt Brecht's* Mahagonny. *Barrows is said to be writing their next effort according to a recent press release and, if insider reports are to be believed, the enigmatic young man with the delicate features that have all club kids abuzz, will bring the group its next hit.*

Becky and I stare at each other. At the article's photo showing James in an absurd pair of tweed pants with suspenders.

Holy crap.

He's going to hate this.

James is pissed, and I'm trying not to be amused.

James is always calm, controlled, polite, in charge. But now he's stomping around my room in his stacked heels, waving the newspaper like a fly swatter.

At least the article is complimentary, I point out.

It makes me sound like a total wanker, he says. His British is escaping, so I know he means it. He asks, Who the hell is going to take someone with "delicate features" seriously as an artist?

I don't remind him of all the bars his looks have gotten him into. I don't remind him of all the auditions his sly smile has won him. I don't remind him of all the times he used his cheekbones to get what he wanted.

The suspenders are cool, though, I say and then duck as the paper comes flying toward my head.

The Howard Johnson's in Times Square has a photographic drink menu. Manhattans and gimlets and things with cherries and oranges and little umbrellas in them.

Becky and I order a load of fried clams to split; James picks

142

at them between sips of his drink. He's been working his way down the cocktail menu, drink by drink, ever since he turned eighteen and got a fake ID. Not that he needs one. People bend over backwards to give James anything he asks for.

Today's choice is something called a rusty nail.

Don't you need to get a tetanus shot for that? Becky asks.

The drink looks watery and strong, and has two cherries bobbing up and down in it like life buoys. I feel guilty because James could go into any nice place he wanted, instead of having drinks in here so we can join him.

Something needs to change, he says. My image or my looks or maybe my next project should be more mainstream, I don't know.

Is this all about that article? I ask.

I glance around to make sure the waitress is far away and then grab one of the cherry stems and bite into the fruit. It squirts in my mouth and tastes like cherry lighter fluid.

James shrugs. I'm just worried about losing time to make my mark.

Look— I say, although I'm not sure what I'm going to point out. Maybe spending your life afraid of something that may or may not happen, is like dying twice.

Thankfully, Becky cuts me off. You know, she says, I don't even know what I'm doing after next year. If I get into college, I have no idea how to pay for it. And if I don't go to school, who will hire me? Not like I have any experience in anything aside from hiding my mom's boyfriends' drugs.

James opens his mouth and closes it. Not even he has anything to follow that up with.

When we walk out, I look up at the life-sized posters hanging in the windows of the Gaiety Male Theatre (NY's NO. 1 SHOW-PLACE, apparently) upstairs from the restaurant. Shirtless boys in bow ties and with top hats and canes.

It's a bit much, but it *is* Broadway, after all.

Becky and Andy are going to the junior prom dressed as Bonnie and Clyde. Connor is back at work and sold Becky a bag of cast-off material for five dollars, and she's made a wild sort of flapper dress. All fringe and beads.

Andy procured a realistic-looking toy submachine gun from somewhere, but his dad confiscated it, saying that it looked too real and could get him shot.

Good thing Clyde's dad never told him that, Andy grumbles.

Yeah, Becky replies, eyes blazing. How awful that all those people wouldn't have been murdered.

Andy leans in to kiss her cheek, and Becky slaps him away. You think he'd know better by now.

I wave Becky and Andy off with a sharp realization that I'll never go to a prom with Gabriel. Hell, I can't even introduce him to my family.

Not that I would introduce him to my parents, anyhow. I like him too much for that.

But I would have liked to take him to prom. Would have liked to see him in a tux. Danced with him to crappy slow songs and fed him meatballs off toothpicks. Drank spiked punch while the teachers milled together in the corner under the guise of supervising.

I would have liked to take him to after-parties and ducked into a side rooms to kiss until we couldn't see straight.

I would have liked to be allowed to have what Becky and Andy are allowed to have.

Time feels heavy, like it's pressing down and I can't stop the questions from pouring out.

Where are you when you aren't here? I ask Gabriel as we huddle in a dark corner at the edge of the bar. Where do you go?

Our cheeks are next to each other so we can hear over the music, and he doesn't pull back when he answers.

I work, he says as though the words are painful.

And then?

And then I work some more. Sometimes I sleep.

Yeah, but...

He shuts me up by moving his lips up to my ear to whisper, And I think about you. But really, Michael, the only thing that matters is the time we're together.

And when I'm with him, it's easy to believe, but I know that five minutes later, I'll be doubting everything again.

We talk about today and next week and next month and next year, and then I have to stop Gabriel to say, I don't even know what the hell I'm going to do after graduation. My parents assume I'll go to college, but I don't know what *I* want.

I know what I want, he says, eyes lidded and dark. Maybe that's enough for both of us.

And then he pulls me to him, and I wonder if it might be.

"Time (Clock of the Heart)" by Culture Club comes on, and we sway together, Boy George's voice circling around us, until Gabriel stops and nudges me to the wall, then steps away, forms his hands into a square and mimes taking a photo.

I want to always remember this time, he says smiling and pointing up at the clock above my head.

Something flutters in my stomach and then rushes to my head. I try not to give in to the hope that anything is possible. That these dark room meetings with Gabriel followed by lies to my parents are enough to make me happy long-term.

But sometimes I can't help it.

Before the room across from mine was filled with boxes of my mother's old clothes and some tools of my father's, and some dishes that Mom brought home after my grandmother died and her house was sold, it was Connor's.

Then, it was filled with comics and punk rock records and bongs so small they could fit in the front pocket of your jeans without anyone noticing. My brother had Yankees posters on the walls, and a hat collection in the closet, and porn under the bed.

Sometimes I go in that room and try to figure out what happened to our family.

I never succeed.

Connor and I are sitting at the diner, and he's picking at a pile of fries. Stacking them crisscross like wood pieces for a campfire.

You're looking better, I say, although I'm not sure if it's true or not. It's hard to tell given that Connor is a pro at making sure his job, or insignificant things like sleep, don't infringe on his social life.

I think again about overhearing him ask for a loan and what my mom said about boys needing their mothers.

Do you want me to talk to Mom? I ask. Seriously, maybe you can move home for a little while, save some money. You know, just until you get caught up or something.

I wait for the smart-ass comeback, the dismissive gesture. But instead, Connor hesitates and then says, Mom isn't the one you'd need to talk to.

You want me to talk to Dad?

No, he says. I'm only pointing out the futility of it.

But you would consider moving home? I ask carefully. I mean, what if your friend comes back and you have to leave the apartment?

Connor turns his face toward the window, the sun highlighting his tired eyes. I have other friends, he says.

Friends who would let you move in with them? I ask before silently reminding myself that I don't want to fight with him.

Yeah, he says, pausing before turning back to me. Then, stronger this time, Yeah.

I think he's delusional, but I don't say anything. Instead, I reach over and grab two fries from the bottom of his pile and watch the rest come tumbling down.

It's over. I'm pretty sure it's over, Becky says. Andy used to hold my hand while we walked down the street. He used to kiss me at stoplights. He used to stare into my eyes and tell me he couldn't imagine being with anyone else. Now, he's on patrol all the time. And when he *is* around, he's always watching over his shoulder. I need to find a way not to love him so much. Not to take our future for granted anymore. We were going to be together forever.

Forever is a stupid word, kitten, James says. Besides, you still have us.

And even to me, his words sound hollow.

Does Andy want to end things? I ask, ignoring James's not-so-hidden dismissive glare.

Becky's anger slides away, but she sounds hurt when she says, No. No, he says we can make it work like his parents do. I just don't know if I want to sit home every night wondering if he's going to come home alive like his mom does when his dad is on patrol. Lord knows I do enough of that with *my* mom.

Why don't you call your mysterious phone number for guidance? James says slyly. The advice it gives you is probably as good as anything Michael and I have to offer.

Becky harrumphs, then says, I'm not going to let some phone dude decide my future.

But after James leaves, she asks if she can make a call and

goes off to the kitchen. Later, I do that *69 thing to redial the last number called. The raspy voice comes on, announces itself, and quotes the Rolling Stones about not always getting what you want, but sometimes getting what you need. I wonder which category staying with Andy falls into for Becky.

I wonder what seeing Gabriel is for me.

My mother asks me to take some boxes to our storage locker. Maybe this is how I'll fill the summer. Moving things around the apartment from one place to another.

I stack the boxes and pull up a flap of the one on top.

Photo albums.

Connor and I as cops and robbers for Halloween, when he was ten and I was almost five.

Me playing guitar at a young performers' showcase at St. Sebastian's.

The four of us at Riverside Park for a picnic.

My dad, with his arm around me at a little league game, his face beaming with pride because I'd pitched a one-hitter. It makes me sad to think he'll never look at me like that again… and then guilty for feeling sad.

I try to remember the last time we were all in the same room and can't. How did we get here?

The glands in Connor's neck are swollen, and he's tired all the time. He says it's nothing. He feels fine. He's been working too hard. Or playing too hard. Or "whatever."

I ask if he thinks he might have mono or Epstein-Barr or something. At least that's the closest I can guess from the pamphlets I grabbed from the nurse's office at school. Connor says he doesn't know, but it doesn't matter because he doesn't have insurance and refuses to go to the St. Mark's Clinic.

I can't go there, he says. It's full of sick people.

I've been checking into the fear room once or twice a week, and even though the same paper is still up, my writer friend hasn't replied.

I'm not overly interested in finding out who the writer is. And I'm not looking to meet someone at school. At the same time, it's nice, for once, not to feel alone.

Today, there are two headlines someone cut out of the *Post* from earlier this month and taped up on the wall. The first reads, "L.I. Grandma Died of AIDS," the second, "Junkie AIDS Victim was Housekeeper at Bellevue."

I'm shocked I didn't hear about those from my dad first.

I rip them off the wall and, behind those, there's new writing in tiny print. The paper is creased in an odd way, so I have to smooth it out in order to see all the words. Of course, I get a paper cut in the process and have to suck the blood off before turning back to see what's written.

I did it once with an older guy upstairs in a club and now I keep checking for spots. Shit. I've gotta be fine, right? I'm about to graduate high school, for fuck's sake.

My hands start to shake, and I pull them back from the paper. Take in a gasp of air, and try not to hyperventilate.

Is this what the rest of our lives are going to be like?

The next time I see Gabriel at Echo, I ask about his past boyfriends.

None, he says.

Really?

None that mattered, no.

But you've been with other guys?

Yeah. And you?

Boyfriends? No.

But others?

No.

Oh, I'd assumed that you and James...

No.

Of course he's been with other guys. No surprise there.

Not like I expected him to be scared like James or looking for a husband like Becky or cautious like me.

Of course he's been with other guys.

Are you angry with me? Gabriel asks over the yearning sounds of Marvin Gaye's "Sexual Healing."

Of course not. Why would I be angry? I answer, only I can't look him in the eye when I say it.

Michael?

I'm not angry. I'm just sick of Danni playing all these freaking love songs.

Michael?

Come on, let's dance.

Before I leave, Gabriel tells me that when he delivered balloons to a synagogue on Park Avenue last weekend, someone gave him a hundred-dollar tip, and he wants to use it to take me to dinner.

I tell him he has to wait until after finals, but then. Yes.

Still, inside I panic. Dinner seems too formal.

This is what I've wanted, I remind myself. A chance for us to actually spend time together outside the club; a chance to get to know who he is in the real world. And so I say yes, because there is nothing else to say.

Gabriel promises to call me with the details, and I'm back to waiting.

For the first time, Connor invites me to join him and his friends at the Gay Pride Parade.

For a second, I consider it. But the whole idea of the parade seems overwhelming. Throw my brother into the mix, and it seems explosive. There is no way that's going to happen.

But the idea of being there sticks in my head.

It won't let go and I figure what the hell, I'll go alone.

I tell my parents I'm meeting Becky at the library to work on a fictitious chemistry final.

When my dad gives me his usual once-over, I have to look away. I'm sure he can read the guilt on my face.

But really, what do I have to apologize for?

Being myself?

I don't tell Becky.

I don't tell James.

I don't see Gabriel again, but I probably wouldn't have told him anyhow.

I *definitely* don't tell Connor.

I avoid the Village, get off the subway in Midtown, and walk over to 5th Avenue as if I were simply going to the big public library.

As I get closer, the crowd gets denser. Louder. Happier. Made more colorful by all shades of clothes and skin and attitudes.

Everyone is singing and clapping and carrying signs. It's like this sea of joy flowing down stuffy 5th Avenue. All these people are so freaking beautiful, I can't even believe it.

Bands march down the street led by half-naked boys twirling batons. The different tunes play over each other in a carnival of sound.

There are gay police officers marching, political groups, some from different neighborhoods and cities, colleges and choirs.

There are even religious groups in the parade, and I wish I had a way of beaming pictures of this to my dad, because I'm pretty sure he'd lose it.

Drag queens are working the crowd. A lesbian group rides up the street on decorated motorcycles, and a group of impossibly hot guys are strutting in gym shorts behind a line of salsa drums.

The parade slows and some parents gather in front of me. I'M PROUD OF MY GAY SON reads one sign, I LOVE MY GAY DAUGHTER reads another.

I guess I always knew parents like that existed, although even Gabriel's dad probably wouldn't have committed to carrying a sign down the middle of Manhattan for the world to see.

But I wonder what it would feel like to have that kind of acceptance.

To not be afraid.

To be fully myself.

For even one day.

WE ARE EVERYWHERE reads one poster.

At school I'm not sure who is gay or who isn't. Here, it's the opposite. I never would have believed that was possible anywhere, much less in the middle of New York City.

For the first time, I feel like I'm exactly where I'm supposed to be.

I step forward to get a better view of a marching band. A cute boy in a tank top, barely older than me, catches my eye, smiles, tosses me a string of gold beads, and keeps walking.

I drape the beads around my neck.

They feel heavier than they are.

The crowd gets bigger, and I try to step up onto the base of a light pole, when an older guy with electric-blue eyes holds out his arm to help me up.

He gives me a look that tells me he knows I'm here alone. That it's my first time.

Maybe next time, you'll be out there marching too, sweetie, he says and smiles.

I hope he's right. I want him to be right. Even just watching from here, I feel free.

Next year I will watch from the Village.

Next year I will march.

Next year I will give myself permission.

Next year I won't only feel free.

Next year I will be free.

When I was little, I used to watch *The Wizard of Oz* every year with my grandmother.

Connor could never sit still that long, but I looked forward to rooting Dorothy on as she tried to get home.

My favorite part was when she arrived in Oz and the movie switched from black-and-white to color.

I used to wonder how Dorothy felt, having her life changed from monochrome to Technicolor so quickly.

Now, I think I know.

It's the last day of school.

I poke my head into the fear room to find one last post. Someone has written, *Love Is...* just like the cartoon in the newspaper. But under that is a list in different writing and pen colors, different people filling in the blank.

Love is...
...all you need
...a battlefield
...Hell
...in the air
...evol spelled backward
...for losers
...the drug
...all around
...all we have left
And I wonder if the answer really matters.
And if that last one is true.
And if it is, if love is even enough.

Becky usually hangs out in the newspaper office at lunch, but they're done for the year, so we sit outside, picking apart some tuna sandwiches.

You've been quiet, she says.

I know, I say. I'm not sure how to talk about it.

Is it your dad? she asks.

Not more than usual.

Instead of playing twenty questions like she usually would, she waits and eventually I start talking about how I felt like a different person at Pride. Like the person I always wanted to be was waiting for a chance to come out, like a genie in a bottle or something.

But isn't that good? she asks.

I know she doesn't get it. Why would she?

Of course it is, I try to explain, But it also sucks because I don't get to be that person in real life and I don't want to go back to pretending. And what I tell her is so fucking true that I start to cry.

I tell her that Nonna, my mom's mom, used to say tears were the language of God.

And I tell her about how my dad always replied that Nonna was going to make sissies of me and Connor. She told us to stand up to him, but we didn't. We learned to bite our lips and hold our breaths, anything not to cry.

But my dad isn't here, and when Becky wordlessly holds out a Kleenex, I let the tears flow.

Things to do:
- → *Finish the paper*
- → *Write a paragraph on the meaning of the book*
- → *Show the timeline of the development of the war*
- → *Run a mile and do pull-ups for the Presidential Fitness Program*
- → *Write out the formula for the chemical equation*

Another school year over.

James is working on his play.

Becky got a summer job selling ice cream at Baskin-Robbins.

Connor has been working nonstop to get the store ready

for a big shipment they're getting in from some old movie star's estate.

I get sick of waiting to hear from B-Sides and go to the store.

The help wanted sign is off the door, and the owner, Mr. Lowenstein, and this girl Tracey who I've seen working there, are hauling empty record bins into the corner of the store.

What are you doing? I ask.

Mr. Lowenstein wipes his forehead and says, CDs. Everyone comes in and sifts through the records, and then they put them away and want to buy little bits of plastic, so I'm making room.

I start to ask about the job, and then Mr. Lowenstein sighs and says, Hopefully the store can stay in business.

Crap. Maybe Becky can get me in at the ice cream place.

I miss that Friday at Echo because their whole block has a water main break.

And I'm not upset. Not really.

It's like I left some important part of myself at Pride, and I don't know how to get it back.

Uh-huh.

That's really all I can say when Gabriel surprises me by calling the next day. He tells me how he can't wait for us to go to dinner, to sit and talk, to spend time together outside the club.

Uh-huh.

We're meeting in Little Italy, at some pasta place Sinatra likes, so it must be good. Seven o'clock.

I hang up.

Who was that? Mom asks.

Just some kids playing around, I say, and then run to the bathroom to throw up before she can ask more.

JULY 1983

Friday night, Becky comes over to give me an excuse.

And to play fashion consultant, apparently.

Blue shirt, she says. It makes the green in your eyes stand out.

This feels…odd.

Why? she asks.

I think about the reasons: I don't know. Is this a date? I mean…it might be, but Gabriel doesn't seem like the dating type, and do guys even date? Does Connor even know what his last boyfriend looked like in daylight?

What I say is, I don't know how to do this.

Michael?

Yeah?

Shut up and put on the blue shirt.

I change in the bathroom. Stare at my reflection in the mirror.

I don't recognize myself.

It isn't the blue shirt, or the fact that my hair isn't sticking up in all directions.

It's that even through the nerves, and the fear, and feeling as though I'm declaring something that can never be taken back, I look happy.

I have a date. In Little Italy. With a boy. His name is Gabriel, and when I'm with him, I want to stop time because he makes me feel…

He makes me feel…

I guess because he makes me feel alive. And he makes me feel like I know who I am.

That's what I want to say to my parents when I leave the house.

James got us free tickets to that National Lampoon movie. I'll be back by midnight.

That's what I *do* say to my parents, despite the fact that James wouldn't be caught dead at that movie, and Becky has plans to see Andy, and from the dismissive look on my father's face, I'm glad I didn't say more.

At some point, there is bread. And salad. And pasta.

At some point, Gabriel orders a jug of wine that comes wrapped in straw, and I somehow don't get carded.

At some point, there are candles that have burned down to tiny white mountains and cake that tastes like coffee.

At some point he looks at me with those dark eyes and says, If I were nicer, I wouldn't be here with you, but I can't seem to stay away, and then laughs in a way that turns me to jelly.

And because of the wine and the candlelight and those eyes, I only hear that he can't stay away, and I'm undone.

Gabriel leads me to a café off MacDougal.

I heard that Jack Kerouac used to hang out here, he says.

I order a cappuccino while Gabriel gets something made with orange juice and sparkling water.

Do you read Kerouac? I ask.

Gabriel smiles in a way that makes his eyes light up. No, he says. But I thought you would.

I keep trying, I say.

But underneath, something bubbles up inside me. I am consumed by the idea that Gabriel thought about what I might read, and figured out I'd like to go somewhere the Beat writers hung out.

Bob Dylan wrote stuff here too, he says, looking over the edge of his glass.

I glance around at the worn wooden tables and the grooved floors and the high rafters. Dylan's gravelly voice floats around and around in my head.

Then Gabriel looks me in the eye and says, Someday, someone is going to take a hot boy to this restaurant and say, Michael Bartolomeo used to hang out here.

I gulp down the rest of my cappuccino so quickly I burn my throat.

He is sweet. And sexy. And…everything.

He is silhouetted against the dark of the sky and the lights of the city.

He is running his fingers under my shirt, and it feels like they've always been there.

He tastes like oranges and salt, words and music, hope and fear and promise.

My entire body feels like a balloon, tethered to him by a string, daring to float away.

Gabriel rides the subway with me and gets off at my stop and walks me to the end of my block.

I have twelve minutes until curfew.

We duck into a doorway and make out in the shadows for eleven and a half of them.

My parents have gone to bed; only I suspect my mother won't sleep until she knows I'm home.

I hear her rustle out of the covers and then quietly close the bedroom door behind her.

Did you have a good time? she asks.

I think, for this one moment when it's just the two of us and my father won't hear, of telling her the truth. Of telling her how full of emotion I feel when I'm with Gabriel, of how complete, somehow. Of how myself.

I think of asking her if she ever felt like this for my father because I can't believe that anyone could. Then she breaks the silence and says my father thinks I'm spending too much time with James, and it isn't that she necessarily agrees, but she feels like she should tell me because, of course, we don't want to upset my father, and I stare at her until she says good night and goes back to her room.

James is on my fire escape.

That's kind of creepy. You know that, right? I ask.

Well, it's not like I let myself in.

He's right. Besides, I'm glad he's here. I climb out and sit next to him. He's wearing a billowy white shirt that he's managed to keep immaculate, even though he's climbed up a flight of dirty iron stairs. There is no way I'm going to tell him about my mother's warning.

Did you have a fabulous time? he asks, handing me a joint. I'm feeling glum, and I was hoping to live vicariously through your torrid love affair.

It's not exactly torrid, I tell him and take a hit, trying not to cough. Although I'm getting to the point that I wish it were.

Why isn't it, then?

Because…I mean, where would we go?

James points to the sky, to the city, lit up like a Christmas tree. He says, Out there. The world is your oyster.

I have a ritual. At the end of every school year, I go through my papers and throw out most of them. Chem tests and history lessons. I keep some of the English papers that don't suck too much, and the occasional art project, even though I draw like a fifth grader. And my report cards.

But I haven't been sure what to do with my results from the career assessment. It seems like the kind of thing that would be cool to find in a box twenty or thirty years from now.

The stack of papers is on my desk as I'm getting ready for bed. The paper clipped to the top is the list I doodled in the margins on.

→ *Fall in love*
→ *Figure out who the hell I am*
→ *Have sex without catching something*
→ *Repair my family*
→ *Escape*

I think I've done the first.

Probably have work to do on the second.

Definitely have work to do on the third.

But, repair my family? Is that even possible? I'm starting to wonder if we're broken, or things were hopeless from the beginning.

And escape? Sure, as soon as I find a place where I can hold Gabriel's hand in the street without worrying about someone threatening to kick the shit out of me.

Do you think there's any chance of fixing things with Mom and Dad? I ask Connor when I see him next. I mean, not as if we were ever the Waltons or anything, but this feels…

Like we're the spawn of a homophobic jackass? Connor fills in.

Really, have you totally given up hope?

Wake up, Michael, he says. If I ever had hope, I gave it up when Dad threw my suitcase off the fire escape.

It's the Fourth of July and I'm pissed because I wanted to go watch the fireworks over the East River, but it's in the mid-nineties again, and it's too hot to breathe much less stand for four hours, crushed up against hundreds of people.

My father is pissed because someone from work promised him Yankees tickets and then reneged, and now Dave Righetti is pitching a no-hitter against the Red Sox.

My mother is probably pissed about something too, only she's too polite or too afraid of my dad to say so.

When my father finally gets around to looking at Saturday's mail, he launches his own fireworks, big enough to rival Macy's.

That's what you get, my father says, throwing my mom's *Time* magazine down on the table. "Disease Detectives," the headline reads. Under that, proving its own point is the only part my father is paying attention to: "AIDS Hysteria."

I pick up the magazine when my father goes back to watching the game. Flip through it. Predictions are that a cure will be found in a couple of years. I wonder if that means we're all safe.

Or if the fear that lives inside my father is like a cancer, and that will kill us if nothing else does.

Before I go to bed, the sound of fireworks ringing through the air, I examine my skin, pink and unmarked, and wonder what I need to give up to keep it that way.

There's a brownout and the voice on Dad's battery-operated transistor radio tells us to ration power.

Outside, the kids from the building across the street have opened some sprinklers and are running through the spray to keep cool. The cops sail by without doing anything; they get that no one wants to run their air conditioner and be the cause of a neighborhood power failure, and it's seriously a furnace inside.

I'm antsy to get out of the apartment and away from my parents, who are bickering about the heat (It's not the heat, it's the humidity, my mom says. I don't give a shit what it is, it's fucking uncomfortable, my dad replies) and the electric bill and some pots and pans that my mom wants to give to Connor, but that my dad wants to throw out.

I tell my mom I'm going to get a Good Humor bar from the bodega and then slip out the door before she can make me a list of things to bring back.

I grab a Coke instead and walk to Riverside Park, and then keep going all the way to the Joan of Arc statue at 93rd, and up to Grant's tomb on 122nd, which is covered in garbage and graffiti and stuff I don't want to examine closely enough to identify.

Two women are standing off to the side, passing a bottle

back and forth. One walks over to me. She's wearing…not much, and not, I don't think, because of the heat.

Hey, she calls, You know who's buried in Grant's tomb?

Yeah, I answer. No one.

When Connor was little, this was his favorite joke because the answer seems obvious, but the remains of Grant and his wife, Julie, are actually in an aboveground building next to the tomb.

Smart boy, she says and moves closer. I like smart boys.

I wonder if I should feel something. Anything.

In books, sixteen-year-old boys are turned on by everything.

Maybe this is a test. Maybe I can avoid the secrets and the dark corners, the fear and the lies. Maybe this is the way to keep my skin unmarked.

But I feel nothing. Nothing at all, except for the weight of the four days and three hours until I have a chance of seeing Gabriel again.

And so I walk away.

I give up on getting a real summer job. Connor's boss pays me to help clean out their storeroom. James asks me to help hang some lights in the theater and even gets approval to pay me for the music I did for the show.

The days move too slowly.

James and Becky and I take turns in front of the oscillating fan in my room, trying to combat the heat.

All art is surrender, James says, as if he's relaying the Yankees score.

Surrender to what? Becky asks.

James pulls on his damp bangs and holds them while he thinks and then answers, Words. Notes. Brush strokes. Anything, really. You have to give up yourself to embrace whatever you're creating, he says, Otherwise, it's just you trying to be artsy.

I like the city best like this, James says. Empty.

I don't understand where everyone goes, Becky replies.

It's easy to see *why* they leave, though. Summer temperatures and steam-filled subways that, on a good day, make everything smell like wet dog.

They go to Europe, James explains. Or the Hamptons. Or Fire Island.

His fingers flutter in front of him. My mother is home and doesn't allow smoking in the house, and he doesn't know what to do with his empty hands. When it gets bad enough, Becky dips into her bag and pulls out a pack of sweet, red-tipped, candy cigarettes. He smirks, but takes them nonetheless, rolling one between his fingers until the paper comes off.

You realize that not everyone can afford to pick up and leave, right? I ask.

James gives me a cocky smile. Of course. Isn't that why we're still here?

AUGUST 1983

Klaus Nomi is dead.

James is sprawled on my floor in the semidarkness.

I never got to meet him, he says. I heard he was playing the Mudd Club last year and waited outside, but the info must have been wrong. Lucy from the theater knew a friend of his and kept saying she was going to try to get him to come to rehearsals, but it never happened.

James sits up and grabs my guitar. He can't play, but silhouetted like this, he looks like a god when he holds it; a young rock star ready to take over the world.

James lucks into a minor G and says, I heard Nomi wore those huge lovely collars to hide the sores. I heard he had it.

It?

AIDS.

But they don't know? I ask.

James glares at me and puts the guitar down gently. Then, in a voice that's anything but gentle, he says, Normal, everyday people are being fired from their jobs, Michael. Do you know how many funeral homes in the city will bury someone who died from AIDS? Guess. No, wait. I'll tell you. Precisely one. I heard Steven's parents wouldn't even visit the hospital to say goodbye because they were afraid of catching something. And of course they didn't tell me, so one of the nicest people I've ever met, died alone.

He takes a deep breath and fights back tears. Then he says, If you were Klaus Nomi, would *you* tell anyone?

James hadn't told me Steven had died.

I feel like the shittiest friend in the world.

People stop at the newsstand and stare, expressions ranging from disgust, to fascination, to awe.

The *Newsweek* cover is the first national publication to show two men together, without hiding the fact that they're a couple, according to the news. It's definitely the first I've ever seen, and I have to shake my head to make sure I'm not imagining it.

But I'm not.

The cover shows two men leaning into each other under letters almost as big as the type in the magazine's name, spelling out GAY AMERICA.

It shows two men looking into the camera and daring the person looking at the magazine to dismiss them.

And yeah, under that is SEX, POLITICS AND THE IMPACT OF AIDS so they're going there, but when I look at the other people milling around to catch a glimpse, there's a kid I've seen at school, who is a couple years younger than me, and he's smiling like he's seeing the most beautiful thing in the world.

Maybe he is.

Later that week, James comes over when my dad is working late and my mom is playing bridge with the women at church. He doesn't want to talk. He won't eat the food Mom left on the counter for me, not even the lasagna.

He stays silent when I suggest hanging out to watch the guys play ball over on West 4th.

He stays silent when I tell him I'm thinking of checking out open mic night.

He stays silent when I tell him about the orthodox Jews I saw coming out of the Adonis movie theater on 8th Avenue, long black coats, long dark sideburns curling into spirals.

Come dancing with me, I suggest and finally get his attention.

I thought you liked to go alone, he says, but his eyes are hopeful.

He's right. I love going downtown and downstairs, and getting lost in the music and the smoke and the smell of sweat and cologne and dry ice. I love—for the length of a song at least—having no name, no history, no fears, no dreams. No reason to want to forget them all.

I like turning to smoke and fading into the room, but can't when James is there. James is a beacon, always drawing me to him.

I do, I say. But this time, I want to go with you. It just has to be somewhere that isn't The Echo, I add, hoping that I don't have to explain.

James looks at me, a complicated response on his lips. But all he says is, Leave it to me. I'll figure something out.

Most of Midtown is dark, thanks to a power line fire, so we go to a party in Battery Park thrown by someone James knows from the theater.

At the entrance, we're stopped by a bouncer dressed head-to-toe in silver glitter, holding some sort of large cat.

She—I think she's a she—leans over and air-kisses James and then whispers something to him in French. He smiles at her. Cat that ate the canary.

What did she say? I ask, eying the tricolored cat who can't take its eyes off James.

She asked if you were my lover, he says. Come on, I need a drink.

You can't escape Madonna, not even here.

While James holds court—he seems to know everyone here; and everyone here, girls, boys, those in-between, or something

174

else altogether, know or want to know him—I dance on my own a few feet away to "Holiday."

This is different than Echo, and not simply because the Friday night crowd there is always a little less adventurous.

The crowd here is older. More glamourous. More intimidating.

But still, I think of Gabriel.

I close my eyes and dance and sway until I could be anywhere. On Mars, even. And when I open them, James is standing next to me, smiling.

What? I ask. It takes me a minute to come back to reality.

I envy you, he says. You've found a way to be content with simply your own company.

Have I? I ask. You sound like Becky's phone guy. What's that supposed to mean, anyhow?

He throws back a shot of something. Sometimes, I wish I didn't need this, he says, waving his empty glass around at the crowd. I wish I didn't need their attention.

I think about trying to explain that I'm not alone because my head is filled with Gabriel, and however much I love playing the guitar and performing, I enjoy my time with him and James and Becky more, and I'd happily never write another song if that meant Gabriel and I would be…something.

But a look in his eyes stops me, and, high on music and life and love, I lean in and hug him instead.

Everyone is drinking champagne, and the liquid is reflecting the lights strung through the trees so it looks as if stars are dying in the glasses.

While we're in line for another round, I overhear a guy with a blond beehive say, I just wanted my freaking teeth cleaned. I mean, I'm not even sick. How could he kick me out like that?

James shakes his head, sobering up, and says, Let's get out of here.

Are you okay? I ask.

James shrugs and says, I don't know.

I wait, knowing James will eventually fill the silence with something of substance.

He sighs and says, Raul had to pull out of the show. His parents wouldn't let him stay in the city any longer. And maybe that makes sense. Maybe none of us should be here.

You'd leave New York? I ask. Where would you go?

James stops and looks up at the spire of the Chrysler Building.

You have a point, he says. Then, under his breath he says, There really isn't anywhere else for me, is there?

I watch the news while I help my mom cut potatoes. Pictures of Pride are being used in some story about research funding, marchers carry a sign that reads WE NEED RESEARCH NOT HYSTE-RIA. Who could possibly argue with that?

My mother coughs. Don't cut yourself, she warns me. I don't want blood on the counter.

I open my eyes and stare at the knife I'm holding. At my hand. Picture my blood running red. Clean.

But what if my blood weren't clean? I guess I could expect the same treatment Steven got.

And even though that's not a surprise, it's damn depressing to think about.

The play that James has been working on all year is finally in dress rehearsals, and he wants us to see it.

I page Gabriel and ask him to come with, but he doesn't call back. I risk calling his home number, but the phone just rings and rings. And even though he said that he and his mom never answer it, even though he warned me not to get too hopeful of ever reaching him by phone, the silence once I hang up sits like a rock in my stomach.

Becky comes over, wearing a dress made of layers of gauze and gloves that go up to her elbows, so I lead her to my room and make an effort, managing real pants and a shirt my mom ironed for me. Becky picks out a skinny tie, rolls up my sleeves, and pulls a stack of stretchy black and white crystal bracelets off her wrist and deposits them onto mine. Then she declares we're ready to leave.

The Space is a couple of blocks from James's apartment, and a couple more from the Hudson River. It's on a block with no streetlamps, and as we walk—past the hookers, past the tough boys in their leather and their sneers, past a group of preppy girls who must have gotten lost on their way in from New Jersey, past a bunch of jocks who follow us for two blocks, talking loudly about how all fags are going to die from this disease and that Becky should leave me for a "real man"—Becky, who is never frightened of anything, grabs my hand and whispers, Andy keeps telling me to carry mace or pepper spray when I'm out on my own. I think this is why.

We're fine, I say loudly and more confidently than I feel. Just keep walking like you belong here.

And that's what we do. Because we belong to the city and the city belongs to us. And we have each other, and Becky is going to try to maybe make things work with Andy, and James is opening a show, and I'm falling in love and done being dismissed, and everything, *everything*, seems possible.

PART

THREE

Blood Makes Noise is plastered on the marquee outside the theater, followed by James's name, the names of two other actors, and that of the director.

We show our school IDs to the guy manning the list at the door and wander into a warehouse-sized space more suited for a parking lot than a theater.

Once we're in, though, it seems fitting. It's obvious that *Blood Makes Noise* is more of an event than a play. There are no chairs. Just open air. Huge speakers. Lights hung everywhere. Curtains on the walls.

And people. People, everywhere.

We mill around until the spots dim.

Then James and the other performers enter the room

from all sides. Each dressed in a single color, they float like a deconstructed rainbow. Sounds screech through the speakers at sometimes ear-splitting levels. A cat's purr. Car horns. Some classical piece. Guitar sounds that I recorded for him. Noises I can't quite recognize. A zipper being pulled, perhaps? A needle dragged across a record. Nails on a chalkboard. Humming. A thunderstorm.

Then silence.

And a heartbeat. Behind everything. That.

Here's the gimmick. Anyone who can stay silent through the entire performance gets their admission refunded. Anyone caught talking is asked to leave.

Performers stop in the middle of the crowd. They're wearing those clip-on mics, and they combine, then break apart and combine again in different combinations to discuss random facts about life. Politics. Sex. Love.

It's kind of like Dial-a-Daze, Becky whispers, trying not to move her lips so we don't get kicked out.

I'm guessing all those facts are from James, I whisper back.

Then silence.

Heartbeat.

Beat. Beat. Beat.

Silence.

From all around us, speakers blare the words, I stay silent…

Then the actors begin to speak, filling in the rest of the sentence:

…*because I don't think anyone will believe me.*

…because I'm not sure I have anything to say.

…because I'm not sure if I'm right.

…because we are at war.

…because I don't know how I feel.

…because no words can explain.

…because I'm tired of arguing.

…because I love you.

The words overlap and get mixed up and tumble around each other until James, in the center of the crowd, ends with: *…because I'm scared.*

The room is hot, but the hair on the back of my neck stands up as if I were outside in January snow. Becky squeezes my hand. She looks at me, puzzled. I'm not sure what to tell her, which is fine since we're not supposed to talk anyhow.

The actors come together, performing small scenes— sometimes only a line or two of dialogue—that end in someone keeping their feelings to themselves. Threats. Attacks. Fights. Illnesses. Politics.

They try to lighten things up a little as well with happier reasons: gifts, pregnancies, votes, love that the person is still coming to terms with.

But just like life, it's the negative stuff that's really intense.

They end with two guys trying to talk about their past sexual experiences before they go to bed together.

I look away so Becky can't see my face. All I'm thinking about is Gabriel.

The question starts again: I stay silent because…

Then the room goes silent.

Then the room goes black.

After a minute that feels like forever, a recording of someone inhaling plays loudly as the lights slowly come up; as if the lights and air are connected.

A girl dressed in yellow dances seductively in front of a group of guys. A boy in green walks around tickling people. James stops in front of us wrapped in blue-gray cloth the same color as his eyes. He hugs us both, then walks over to a girl dressed in lace, dips her, and spins her around. When he's done, she stumbles back, flushed, dizzy. He moves on, stopping in front of random people. Daring them to speak.

Around us, people laugh. Someone screams. A boy's stomach gurgles. A girl coughs. One by one, they're picked out of the crowd and taken out of the theater as punishment for their transgressions. Only the quiet ones stay to the end.

By the curtain call, Becky and I are standing with only a handful of survivors. Those who, for better or worse, have kept silent.

We wait by the stage door, and when James comes out, Becky elbows her way through the crowd and throws her arms around him like she never wants to let go.

He's flushed and his long hair is damp against the top of his collarless jacket. He catches my eye and I feel like I need to say something, but "good show" isn't going to cut it. And speaking still seems taboo, which I think he understands, because when he extricates himself from Becky and reaches out a hand to squeeze my shoulder, he only nods.

We assume that, like he always does after a show, James will head out with the cast to review the performance. Becky and I walk toward the subway, with only the sound of her boot heels to accompany us.

Finally, I break the silence. Well, that was intense.

Yeah, she replies so quietly her voice is almost lost in the street noise.

Then the silence wraps tightly back around us and there's nothing left to say.

When we hear from James a couple days later, Becky and I race to meet him at Howard Johnson's where, instead of a cocktail, he orders a Jameson on the rocks.

Whiskey? Becky asks, looking at the clock. It's eleven thirty in the morning.

James wraps his hands around the glass and says, Well, it's five o'clock somewhere.

The show, I start. That was intense.

Becky interrupts. What I want to know, she asks, is whose heartbeat was it?

James gives her a cockeyed look and says, Mine. Why?

Becky laughs and says, Of course it was; I thought it sounded melodramatic.

This at least makes him smile. Then our plate of clams arrives, and Becky says something snarky about her mom, and we pretend everything is back to normal.

Becky leaves first.

James has had a little too much whiskey.

So have I, because he's been pouring half his drinks into my Coke.

What is it that you're so scared of? I ask him.

He shakes his glass and stares at the ice cubes crashing together. Everything, he says, under his breath. Then, before I can process it, Come on, let's get out of here.

It's a relief to go to The Echo the next weekend and try to forget the world. Someone has a Polaroid camera, and the whole night, people line up to have their pictures taken for a buck, with the money being donated to Gay Men's Health Crisis (GMHC). I feel like I haven't seen Gabriel in a lifetime, and I can't get enough of the sound of his voice, his scent, his fingers on the back of my neck.

We wait our turn, swaying back and forth to Modern English singing, "I Melt With You." I'm high on the whole night, with Gabriel's arms wrapped around me, and the lights and the music and my hands in the air. I feel like I can fly. I feel defiant.

Then it's our turn and we stand in front of the camera, and I can't stop laughing until Gabriel leans in and sings along to the music about how there's nothing we won't do and stopping the world to melt together and then I'm not sure how to breathe.

I float home on a trail of his words.

But then realize I don't have the photo with me.

Damn.

Blood Makes Noise opens, and the next morning, we run to the newsstand at the corner of 86th and Broadway and wait for the papers to be delivered so we can read the reviews.

James is wired and talking about how twelve blocks of the garment district near Macy's have no power and won't until next week and how all the cops have been pulled over there and Mayor Koch has invited any fabric buyers for market week to a party at Gracie Mansion if they stick around.

I tune him out and watch as Becky rummages around in the coin return of the pay phone and pulls out a quarter. James stops talking and shakes his head in disgust. Really, kitten, he says, I'd happily give you money if it will keep you from sticking your hands in there.

She's about to reply when the newspaper delivery truck pulls up.

The three of us freeze in mirror poses as the papers land on the curb with a loud *thunk*. We stay frozen as the clerk cuts the twine around the bundles with a pocket knife. As he pulls yesterday's old paper off the shelves and replaces them with today's.

James moves first, pays, and hands the paper to me. I rifle through the pages and then scan the article quickly.

This time there is no mention of James's cheekbones. This time there is no photo of him in suspenders. This time there are only words, and the ones that stand out are these: Important. Stunning. Necessary.

Becky pulls us both into a hug and doesn't let go.

I can feel James relax. The tightness in his arms loosen.

For all of the shit that she and James give each other, this is who we are.

Becky Kaplan is our heart. James Barrows is our soul.

At some point, I need to figure out what role I play.

Gabriel isn't at Echo when I get there, but Brian waves me over to the bar and hands me an envelope.

What's this? I ask.

I don't read 'em, I just deliver 'em, he says, and starts washing some glasses that are still stacked up from the night before.

I move to the wall. Hold the envelope up in the blue light. Examine my name written in straight, sharp letters. A thin knife of a line scored underneath.

I feel something that resembles possibility. As if anything could be written inside. But then doubt kicks in. It could be bad news. Or a joke.

I rip open the envelope and slice my finger along the edge.

A quick drop of blood forms, and I suck it away before anyone can see.

At the moment, a gun would cause less panic in New York City than a gay boy bleeding.

My finger wrapped in a napkin, I pull the photo from the envelope.

The Polaroid girl caught me staring up into the lights. Next to me, Gabriel is all muscles and innuendo, and he's looking at me as if I've said something profound and interesting.

I flip the photo over and read, in Gabriel's loopy writing,

Worth stopping the world for.

There was "before Gabriel" and there's "now." Places and times in my life he didn't fit into, and places defined simply because I knew he existed.

I was seeing him. I'd just seen him. I was counting the days until I could talk to him to decide when I was seeing him next.

How do you know when you're in love? I ask, although I suspect I know the answer because I know how I feel when I'm with Gabriel.

It isn't love, Becky says. You just want to get into his pants and he just wants to get into yours, and I'm not even sure that love exists.

You don't have to be so cynical, James says.

Becky glares at him. Oh, what do you know? she asks and storms out of the room.

My parents are going out of town for two days.

Thirty-two hours to be exact, but that includes a night. An entire night.

191

My mother says, I guess you're old enough to stay on your own, but you'll remember to call your brother if you need anything?

Sure, I'll call my brother, I think. Either it will take him two weeks to call me back because he's out with his friends, or he'll make plans with me and stand me up anyhow.

Of course, I say to her. Nothing to worry about.

I take more soup to Connor's as a ruse for having a quiet place to make a call and figure that he'll at least have something to eat in the apartment.

Can I use your phone?

What are you up to? he croaks from the couch, shielding his eyes from the sunlight I've invited into the room by committing the cardinal sin of opening the curtains.

Can I use your phone or not?

He waves at the wall in the kitchen. Yeah, whatever.

I wait for the apartment's radiator to stop clanging and then dial, counting the rings that tell me Gabriel isn't going to answer.

But just as I'm getting ready to hang up, he comes on the line, voice groggy.

I glance at the clock. Half past two.

Did I wake you? I ask. Hard night?

Then I blush when I hear him stretch and say, It would have been if you'd been here.

I want to ask what he did to still be sleeping. And who he was doing it with. But those aren't questions he ever answers, so

I swallow them and clear my throat. Listening for any sign that Connor has moved from his perch of pillows to eavesdrop.

My parents are going out of town this weekend, I say into the phone. And I owe you dinner.

Dinner?

Well, you took me out and all, I remind him. And, I mean, we'd have the house to ourselves.

Well, then… Gabriel lets the sentence fade into a smile I can hear over the line.

Yes, I answer. Well, then.

In the living room, Connor is curled up on the couch, flipping through an old copy of *TV Guide*. From the cover, the cast of *M*A*S*H* wave goodbye. Smiling as if the war was some game, which I guess it was to them. They're only actors, after all.

Are you sure you aren't sick? I ask. I mean, he must be if he wasn't putting a glass up against the room divider to try to listen to my call or even giving me a hard time about it.

Nah, too much to drink last night. Destiny had a show.

Destiny? I ask. The one who can't be bothered to walk upstairs?

Don't judge. Would you want to walk up five flights of stairs in six-inch stilettos?

I stare at him, relieved that everything is back to normal. Kind of.

Seriously, Michael, I'm good, he says weakly.

Sure you are, tough guy. Remember that the next time you want me to schlep Mom's soup from the Upper West Side.

In an odd surge of brotherly camaraderie, I pull out the photo of me and Gabriel from my bag and pass it to Connor.

What magazine did you tear *this* out of? he asks, smirking.

Funny, I tell him. That's Gabriel. Then I wait, oddly wanting my brother's approval or at least an acknowledgment we're on the same page for once.

Connor stares as the photo and says, He looks…

Then he stops and bends the photo in the light before saying, Hot. And familiar. He looks familiar.

I promise you don't know him, I say, grabbing the picture and putting it back into my bag. But I'm pretty sure I'm paler than my brother now. I refuse to believe in any reality where Connor would have crossed paths with Gabriel.

As I'm cleaning up, I come across a small printed booklet. How TO HAVE SEX IN AN EPIDEMIC: ONE APPROACH, the cover reads.

The table of contents makes me squirm with equal measures of curiosity and fear.

But my parents are leaving town.

And Gabriel is coming over. So curiosity wins out.

The opening pages explain that since no one knows exactly how someone gets AIDS, no one can know for sure how to avoid it. It says while some people will give up sex altogether—I guess James isn't alone with his fear—the pamphlet was written assuming most gay men reading it would want to find a way to have sex without getting sick.

I flip back and forth from the table of contents to the relevant pages: Kissing. Sucking. Touching.

All the things we might do.

My face on fire, I skim the booklet, wondering how much I can learn in the five minutes before my brother wonders where I am. What I'm doing. What I'm imagining.

It discusses how to talk to a potential partner. Estimating risk.

Knowing your partner isn't the issue, it stresses. Neither is the number of partners you have. The issue is the disease.

Maybe James is the smart one. Maybe fear is the only thing that makes sense. But thinking about Gabriel reminds me that I'm not James. *He* might not want to have sex, but it's occupying my mind more and more, and I'm desperate to know what this thing is that people have killed for, died for, loved for.

What sticks in my head is: talking, washing, condoms, protect yourself, stay alive.

Before I leave, I take a good long look at Connor curled up on the couch.

Is he really hungover? Not like *that's* out of character.

Is it too late for him to take what that pamphlet had to say seriously? Does Connor ever take anything seriously?

Have you thought about moving home? I ask him again, instead. At least there, I could keep an eye on him.

Have you thought about pushing me in front of the F train? he asks, leaning his head back into the pillows. It would be less painful.

On the way home, I pass a pay phone and then turn back and pull a quarter out of my pocket.

I know you can't simply call some random number and get advice. It's like following horoscopes in the newspaper. Everyone in the world born in the same month doesn't have the same life. And everyone who calls Dial-a-Daze doesn't either.

And I don't even have one specific question I need answered; I have many of them.

Is my brother going to be okay?

Am I ever going to feel like I have a family again?

Will Gabriel and I ever have sex? Am I stupid for wanting it more than being afraid of it?

It's like those ridiculous Magic 8-Balls and all I ever get are the little triangles that say: "Ask again later."

But twenty-five cents seems like a small price to pay on the off chance, so I call.

This is the future, the recording says. *Your future. A week ago, you might not have recognized the person you are today. A week from now you might be different still. Savor this time. Be proud of who you are at this singular moment.*

Have I changed so much in the last week?

Will I change in the next?

Will a night with Gabriel and whatever we do or don't do change me that drastically?

Will anyone else be able to tell?

Next, I duck into St. Sebastian's.

I don't remember the last time I prayed for anything.

Please, I whisper, please let Connor be okay.

Blood Makes Noise has been extended from its original limited run.

How come you don't seem happier about it? I ask James while Becky paints his nails an absurd shade of green.

He pulls his hand back, earning a scowl from Becky. It isn't that I'm unhappy about the show doing well, he says. It's definitely nice to know how I'm spending the next few months. I'd just rather not feel like I was capitalizing on people's fear in order to do it.

James's eyes linger on mine, and I realize how difficult it has to be for him to get up there every night and talk about fear: his and everyone else's.

My parents leave in four days.

I wrestle with the idea of telling Becky that Gabriel is coming over to spend the night. More with the idea of telling James. But then, we decide to head to Howard Johnson's, and when we get there, I tell them both.

You need a safe word, Becky says.

What?

James swallows a laugh. She means you need a word so when your tryst gets to be too much and you're screaming "no" and really mean "no" that he'll believe you're serious.

197

It isn't like that, Becks, I say.

But really I guess I don't know what Gabriel is into.

I put my head down on my arms. This is a mistake, isn't it? I ask, but I'm not sure if I mean Gabriel coming to my house or my telling James and Becky that he's coming to my house. But of course they assume that I'm asking a real question about Gabriel coming over.

Becky says, Maybe. James shrugs and says, Well, you *could* just rent a movie and lie around on the couch together.

Then he says, Oof, when Becky elbows him in the ribs.

Look, kitten, it never pays to be too safe now, does it?

If you two could maybe stop for five minutes, I'm serious here, I throw in.

I'm serious too, Becky says. And, as much as I hate to admit it, James actually makes a good point.

James places his hands over his heart and swoons dramatically. Good lord, he says. Did you hear her? The world is ending.

I cross my arms and wait. It's a toss-up as to whether they're more annoying when they're arguing or agreeing.

Speaking of safety… Look, I get it. It isn't like you're going to get pregnant or anything, Becky says as the waitress stops by with more water.

James busts out laughing, while I try to sink under the table.

Anyhow, Becky continues, voice thankfully quieter. Andy's mom says as far as they can tell, the best way to reduce risk is to avoid taking in any bodily fluids. So don't get caught up in the moment, Michael. I'd like you not to die.

I think I stop breathing for a moment, but then mumble, Sorry, I opened my mouth. But it's too late for Becky to let this go.

Right, James? she asks, calling in reinforcements. Tell Michael that I'm right.

James, pale, fiddles with the tiny straw in his drink and looks down at the table when he says, She's right, Michael. We don't want you to die.

Becky gets suddenly serious and suddenly pissed off. Really? she says, narrowing her eyes at James. You, of all people.

Me of all people, what? What does that mean? he asks, looking up.

Becky throws her hands in the air and says, Oh, never mind. Michael, make sure you and Gabriel have condoms, just in case. Seriously, I don't know what I'd do if anything happened to you.

Here I thought I was asking their opinions on what to make Gabriel for dinner. Not about buying condoms, or using condoms, or really even about needing them, although I guess that's what this is all about, when it all comes down to it. Barriers.

SEPTEMBER 1983

My mother keeps me busy running errands. Pick up their dry cleaning. Go to the post office. Bring home the groceries so she can make the food I can't tell her I'm not going to eat while she's gone.

With two days left, I'm climbing the walls. When I can finally sneak away, I visit Becky at work.

The minute the store is empty, she goes to the back room, digs into her army bag, the one with alternating checkerboard Canal Jeans buttons and rainbow Unique Boutique ones, and pulls out a small package wrapped in blue and tied with a green ribbon.

Open it later, she says. Not around your parents.

I poke the tissue paper and recognize the shape more from magazine ads than personal experience.

I wonder if everyone's best friend buys them condoms.

I needed an excuse to go into that store in the Village anyhow, she explains, and I knew you'd chicken out. I was insatiably curious.

Sure she was; she probably isn't lying. And before I can ask about her visit to the sex shop, and what she bought, and who she intends to use it with because Andy hardly seems like the type, a woman comes in with five whining kids, and I back out of the store with only a wave.

Do I call Gabriel to confirm?

Make sure he hasn't lost my address?

Make sure he's still going to be here at three?

Make sure I haven't lost my nerve?

My parents leave at one o'clock.

I change my sheets, throw my old stuffed frog into the closet, make sure the dishes are done, and that my father's REAGAN FOR PRESIDENT: LET'S MAKE AMERICA GREAT AGAIN poster is off the wall and stashed away in the back closet. Then I take the longest, hottest shower ever.

The clock reads two thirty.

I pace for thirty minutes.

The buzzer sounds.

I hit the button without saying anything.

And wait for what feels like years for him to come up from the lobby.

Gabriel knocks on the door. I open it, and then we stand there staring at each other.

It's surreal to see him outside the context of the club, even more in the doorway to our apartment.

He smiles and walks in. Backpack slung over his shoulder.

I look around and try to see the living room the way he must. It's too green, with its wallpaper left over from the previous owners, and the bookshelf that's bending under the weight of my mother's glass bird collection, and the old family Christmas photo over the TV with me and Connor in matching sweaters that has been there so long I usually don't notice it.

Everything in me screams to grab Gabriel's arm and pull him out of here as fast as I can. Instead, I take his bag and set it down next to my father's chair. When I turn back, he pulls me into him and kisses me long enough to make me dizzy.

And I know I'll never look at this room the same way again.

We head to my room. Gabriel tosses himself down on my bed and stretches out as if he's always been there.

His eyes travel over my desk, my old baseball trophies, a stack of dusty cassettes, a postcard from when Becky went to Disney World as a nanny for some friend of her aunt's. They land almost audibly on my guitar.

Play something for me, he says, in a voice that makes me shiver. You owe me one for that tumbling run in Washington Square.

I freeze, wondering why I left the guitar out. Why I'm nervous to play for him when I know I don't suck and I've dreamed of playing for him so many times.

I force myself to pick it up, check the tuning, and strum the opening to a Simon and Garfunkel song.

I still have this idea about writing a song for Gabriel, but every time I go to add a lyric, I come up with another question about him I don't know the answer to.

I don't want to think about that tonight. The worrying gets to me enough when Gabriel isn't here; I don't want anxiety to ruin the time when he is.

I look up and he's hanging upside down off my bed, watching me with a ridiculous smile on his face.

Worth stopping the world for, he says.

And then:
- → *We kiss in my bedroom*
- → *Kiss in the living room*
- → *He runs his hands under my shirt in the kitchen*
- → *I return the favor in the hallway*

When he runs his hand up and down my thigh, time does this weird erratic thing that makes me feel like Dr. Who, whizzing around in a British police box. It's been seconds. It's been years. I'm dizzy like I've been dancing under strobes for too long. Like I've been holding my breath and no longer need oxygen. Like I've learned to breathe nothing except Gabriel.

Let's go out and get some air, Gabriel says.

I'm sure the look on my face translates into, *What the hell are you talking about? What have I done wrong? Why am I the only one who doesn't want to stop?*

Obviously Gabriel still needs oxygen, and that kind of sucks.

I nod, though, because he's smiling his crooked smile and because I don't want him to think I only want to mess around and not actually spend time with him.

I don't want him to think of me like that.

Even if I am.

Like that.

A little.

I splash some water on my face, and we go out to get some stuff for dinner. I could heat up Mom's lasagna, but I want something different. Something sexier. Something my mom hasn't had her hands on.

It's five blocks to Zabar's, a supermarket that my parents can't even afford to shop in. We careen through the aisles. Cheese. Pâté. A box of black-and-white cookies. Gabriel buys a six-pack of wine coolers. I buy half a pound of Jordan almonds for no other reason than that there's something I find kind of sexy about letting the colored sugar dissolve in my mouth. I can barely handle the idea of it dissolving in his.

Just thinking about it makes me stumble up the curb at Broadway, untying the lace on my right shoe. I stare at it, my hands filled with bags.

Wait, Gabriel says. He puts his packages down on the street and kneels, retying the laces. Before he stands, he looks up at me and smiles.

I'm sure I'm blushing in a million shades of red, but all I can think is *yes*.

We spread the groceries out on the table. Bumping into each, apologizing awkwardly, then doing it again.

And we talk.

Becky is going to ask me what we talked about, so I try to commit the topics to memory.

Gabriel took his sister to the Bronx Zoo. The polar bear was her favorite.

He asks me to tell him about Connor. I try, but fail to describe the contradictions that are my brother.

I take an almond, coated in pale blue sugar, and boldly put it in his mouth. I think about the sugar dissolving and about how I might, as well.

Reading my mind, he leans forward, transfers the now-naked almond to my tongue. I'm on fire.

The phone rings, and we pull apart as if a yellow cab just sped through the living room.

At first, I don't move to get it. I mean, how can I?

But when Gabriel says, What if it's your parents? I wander over to the phone in the living room in a daze, pick it up too late, and hear only the click of someone hanging up.

I glance at the clock, watch it tick away my time with Gabriel. We have another twelve hours. Maybe fourteen. It's like the minutes are turning to liquid and seeping through the cracks in the floor into the Hendersons' apartment downstairs.

When I head back to the kitchen, Gabriel is standing at the sink with his wet shirt in his hand. The muscles in his back handcuff my eyes and won't let go.

I spilled some coffee on it, he explains, and turns back to the sink to rinse it out.

A subway rumbles by, and I'm glad it's loud enough to cover up the sound of my jagged breathing.

I take a step forward, unsure what to do.

Gabriel glances over his shoulder and asks what I'm thinking, and I'm sure I turn bright red again because what I'm thinking is that I'm wondering what he sleeps in or out of. What he looks like at dawn when the sun wakes him up. What the stubble on his cheek would feel like against my neck.

I want to see him disarmed, unguarded.

Naked.

I'm not going to tell him that, so I shrug. But then he turns, leans over, runs a finger down the side of my face. I move in to kiss him, but he pulls back and whispers, I mean it. I want to know what you're thinking. I want to know how it makes you feel when we're together. How you feel when I do this, he leans over and blows on my neck.

My breath comes out uneven, my muscles taut as guitar strings.

What does it feel like? It feels like I've turned to smoke.

It feels like everything.

When I don't answer—can't answer—Gabriel snaps me with his shirt and walks to my room to get a new one from his bag.

I've screwed this up. I should have asked Connor… No, not Connor. I should have asked Becky more questions or James or bought some magazines. Or *something*. There is no way I'm going to be able to hide the fact that I have no idea what I'm doing.

When Gabriel comes back in a blue T-shirt and starts throwing food together, I'm too keyed up to eat.

Then he glances at the clock and asks to use the phone.

I'm puzzled until he says, I try to call Sophia to say good night if I'm not there to put her to bed. Ever since Papa died, she has nightmares.

Of course, I say. He stretches the phone into the living room and calls. Murmurs in Spanish in a tone of voice I haven't heard him use before.

It feels wrong to be so damned turned on by his devotion to his little sister.

After dinner, I take the phone off the hook. I can always tell my mom I forgot to put it back and deal with the fallout later.

We head to my room, and I stare at my boom box.

I should have made a tape.

Music for losing your virginity.

Safely. Of course.

Whatever that means.

At least I know where the condoms are. Not that I want to start with anything that needs condoms. At least I don't think I do.

I put on Echo and the Bunnymen and then pull the tape and play Spandau Ballet, "True."

Gabriel wraps his arms around me, and we're dancing so slowly that we're barely moving, and I can feel him hard against me and it's the sexiest, most wonderful, most terrifying thing ever.

He dances us over to the bed and looks into my eyes.

I think he's going to say something about how much he wants me, how good he feels or something.

Instead, he says, I hope you don't mind if we use condoms. I've been with a lot of guys, and I want to keep you safe.

My heart stops.

The night bleeds away.

We lie in my bed, which has never felt so small, and I can feel my pulse beating as loudly as the bass leaking in the window from the cars stuck at the light outside.

I know that star, Gabriel says, pointing up at the ceiling.

Well, it *is* yours, I choke out.

Michael, he says. Talk to me.

I sit up. Look at the unopened condoms on the nightstand. Rake my hand through my hair. How many is a lot? I ask before I can stop myself.

We sit on my floor drinking coffee laced with my mom's cooking brandy. Me out of a Yankees' mug of my dad's (if *he* only knew), while Gabriel's hands are wrapped around one from St. Sebastian's (if *they* only knew).

Gabriel is in gray sweatpants and no shirt, and when my tired eyes keep straying to his abs, I tear them away to watch the twenty black jelly bands he twists on his wrist as he tells me that yes, he's been with a bunch of guys, but no, he doesn't have anything, and that when he was talking about being safe he was really thinking about gonorrhea or something as if that's supposed to make me feel better.

I know you haven't been with anyone, he says. I only wanted to make sure we were careful.

I know, I say.

And I do. This is exactly what that pamphlet talked about. Caring about someone means wanting to keep them safe. Wanting to keep yourself safe. I can't blame Gabriel for that. But I can't form those words out loud, either.

Thank you, I say. But...

Michael, he says. I want to be with you. Not just for sex; you matter to me.

My pulse races again with his words, but then he leans up to kiss me, and I pull back without thinking. But you've been with a lot of guys just for sex, I repeat. My voice comes out in a monotone.

I think of him hanging out at the type of places that Connor goes to. Think of him at the parties and at the baths.

And I'm so damned conflicted because he's only living his life.

But...

210

This is different than watching a memorial in Central Park.

This is different than watching someone interviewed on television.

This is different than James worrying about the people he knows, although I think I get his fear now.

This is Gabriel—my Gabriel—no, not mine. Gabriel who has slept with a lot of guys, and who the hell knows if even one of them is sick?

Do you want me to leave? he asks.

My thoughts are spinning as fast as a disco ball, a whirling dervish, a tornado.

He isn't sick. I trust him when he tells me that. At least I think I do.

But that could change. The being sick part, not the trust.

Or maybe that too.

I don't want a life dictated by fear.

But I'm not an idiot.

I'm half in love with him. More than half.

But at the moment, I'm not sure I want to be.

Talk to me, Michael. Talk to me, he says over and over in so many ways. But I'm empty of words. Empty of everything.

His eyes are on the floor.

I've never seen Gabriel without his swagger. It makes him

211

look young. It makes me want to put my arms around him and tell him it's all okay. But I don't know how to make it okay.

After he dresses and packs, he stares at me as if he wants me to say something to stop him.

You don't have to go, I try. But my voice doesn't sound anything close to sincere.

He pauses at the door, bag slung over his shoulder, gives me a sad smile.

I'll see you around, I hope, he says and walks out, leaving me with an unconsummated kiss on my lips. I'm left with only the sound of blood rushing through my veins overlaid on top of the silence. So much silence.

I pace. Trapped.

Is this how James feels? Is this the fear that he's letting dictate his life? Am I stuck with this too, then?

Is fear just another type of disease?

I never should have invited Gabriel over in the first place. What was I thinking, anyhow?

I miss him. I want him.

What if he calls?

I turn the phone ringer back on.

Why did I let him leave?

The phone rings, and I hold my breath.

If Gabriel asks to come back, will I let him? What do I say?

I don't know, but I race to answer before he gives up.

Only, it isn't Gabriel.

I know where I've seen your boyfriend before, my brother says. Ask him about the back room at Beat Box.

My mouth goes dry, and I hang up without uttering a sound.

When I was nine and Connor was thirteen, my parents went to a convention my dad's company was holding in New Jersey. It was the first time I remember them leaving us at home together for a whole day.

As soon as they left, we parked ourselves in the living room, watched tons of bad TV, and ate everything we could find in the kitchen despite having promised Mom to only have sandwiches and two of the Jiffy Pops she'd left out on the counter for us.

Then, it started to rain and got dark. Connor was excited to be in charge, and I was nervous to be left alone with only my brother, but I couldn't tell him that, so I kept to my room, listening to records and reading Archie comics.

Connor wanted to snoop through Mom and Dad's bedroom, but I was too afraid to get caught and I started to cry; only Connor made fun of me, so I locked myself in the bathroom and he couldn't get the door open and I had to stay there until my parents came home.

I feel the same way now, and I have to get out.

I pack my brother's words away in the back of my head and take a chance, showing up at James's apartment without calling, which is dicey because it's not like he's ever home.

But I guess not everything can go wrong at once. When I call from across the street, James is the one to pick up the phone.

I manage a strangled, Can I come up? And when I reach the door, James is already there.

We stand, frozen. James looks concerned and I feel jittery, as if I've been pushed onto the third rail.

I search for something profound to say to explain my showing up with no warning, for showing up at all.

James brushes his hair out of his eyes and looks me over. Five years from now, you won't even remember this day, he says and pulls me upstairs.

James makes tea, gives me a joint, pulls the curtains, and puts some hypnotic Eno album on his turntable.

He dims the lights and says, We can talk or not. Your call.

I inhale deeply and imagine the smoke searing what's left of my heart. When I exhale, I fumble through the story in a burst of blue haze.

James hesitates. What exactly is it that you're upset with him for? he asks carefully.

I know it's a valid question, even if I don't want to think my anger might be caused by hurt feelings. Did I want Gabriel sitting home waiting to see me and no one else?

I can't be mad at him for the condoms, I say. I had some too.

I don't tell James they were a gift from Becky, but I do say: I had them, just in case. You know. Because it seemed like the right thing to do, but I didn't really think of him as someone who might need to use them because…

Disappointment, James says. You had this idea of how things would go and that changed.

But what if one of the guys he's fooled around with is sick? I say as I watch the smoke dance around the ceiling, What if he's caught something? What if condoms aren't enough, anyhow? What if even kissing someone is enough to get infected?

James pauses, and I expect him to say something along the lines of, *Well, then, we're all fucked.* But instead, he quietly says, And now you understand where I am.

Is it horrible that I still think I'm in love with him? I ask after a minute.

Of course not. Besides, ultimately, everything is about love, James says, taking the joint from me. He takes a hit, then stubs it out, says, Friends. Family. Even art.

You really think so? I ask, the pot making me brave.

Sometimes I think I'm in love with the whole world, he says, looking up at me through his lashes as if he's confessing something. Maybe that's part of the problem, I'm terrified of missing out on what comes next. When I heard about Steven...

It's like it's real now, I interrupt.

It was always real, Michael. Don't fool yourself.

I know the joint has gone to my head, but still I'm aware James and I have never spoken this way before. Not really.

He fiddles with a strand of crystal beads around his wrist and says, The way I look at it, you have your sights set on someone who cares enough to try to protect you. There are worse things.

215

The hitch in his voice makes me wonder if Steven knew he was sick and almost had sex with James, anyhow. And what that would have meant.

I do admire Gabriel, James continues, for being honest with you, but I'm the last person who can tell you what to do.

I try to decide whether I agree with James or not. Maybe out of everyone, he's actually the best person to tell me what to do. Before I can argue, though, James shrugs and says, Perhaps you should be asking Becky, and then we both dissolve in sad, stoned laughter.

I go home. I have to go home because if I'm not there when my parents get back, who knows what will happen.

But everything has changed. I see Gabriel's indentation on my pillow. Find his hair in the shower. Smell his soap on my sheets.

And I realize that even Echo is off limits until I get my head together.

Where is left for me?

I avoid the phone. But every time it rings, I *69 it to see who called, knowing there will be hell to pay when my parents get the bill.

Connor.

Connor.

A number I don't recognize.

And finally, Gabriel.

None of them leave messages, so I make up fake ones in my head from Gabriel, like *I'm sorry. I was joking, I'd never sleep with random guys "just for sex" when I knew I was going to be seeing you.*

Then the me in my head gets mad at the Gabriel in there. *You weren't supposed to turn into my brother*, I yell. *You should have figured this out before you came up to me at the club. Before you kissed me and asked me out and came to spend the night with me.*

And then I get mad at myself, because who am I to tell him to get his shit together when I can't deal with my own?

My parents aren't due back for another four hours. I waste two of them watching shit TV and pretending to play guitar.

I wish I was one of those people who could turn pain into art, but I can't play well when my mind is a mess.

Then there's a sharp knock on the door.

My mind races. James went to rehearsal. Becky wouldn't come over knowing that Gabriel was supposed to be here. Maybe it's Mrs. Wyatt from down the hall, checking to see if my mom can watch her cat.

I try to ignore it, but the pounding continues.

I drag myself up and open the door without even looking through the peephole, almost hoping it's some deranged killer who can put me out of my misery.

What the hell, dickhead? my brother says. How many freaking times do I need to call before you answer the phone?

I don't want a lecture, particularly not one from Connor,

but before I can slam the door closed, he's pushed himself into the living room.

Dad isn't back yet, right? he asks, his eyes shifting as if he's realizing all of a sudden that this could have gone badly for him.

What do you want? I ask, turning and retreating to my room.

Connor follows and stands blocking the doorway with his outstretched arms. He looks better than he has in weeks. Healthier. Taller, if that's possible. I realize it's been actual years since he's been in the apartment. For all of my comments about him moving home, I'm not sure he even fits here anymore. It's like he's too big, too loud, too Connor.

What do you want? I ask again as he scans the room, looking for changes. Or perhaps looking to see what's stayed the same.

I wanted to keep you from doing something stupid, he says. Did you screw him?

You can leave at any—I start to say, but Connor pushes me up against the back of the door, my hanging robe thankfully cushioning the blow.

I'm not messing around, he yells, face scrunched up, way too close to mine. Answer me, he demands. Did you have sex with him?

I push my brother back as hard as I can and walk under his arm. Man, I say, going for the jugular, you sound just like Dad.

This stops him as I knew it would. I can see his legs shake, the blood drain from his face, his breath hitch.

Don't be a little shit, Michael, he says, but his quivering voice doesn't match the force of his words.

He walks over and sits on my bed, leans over elbows to knees.

Please, please, please, tell me you didn't have sex with him, my brother pleads. That you didn't let him have sex with you.

Since when do you care about my sex life? I ask, wishing I had a sex life for him to care about. Or not to care about. Whatever.

He rubs the back of his neck and looks at the floor when he answers, Since my little brother is chasing the ass of someone I saw go in the back room at Beat Box a few months ago with Matt Sloan. And since Matt Sloan died yesterday in the fucking AIDS ward at fucking St. Vincent's.

I walk into the living room to try to clear my head. My stomach threatens to puke up the coffee that's still floating around in there.

Gabriel isn't sick, I say to Connor who has followed me, but it's hard to hear any conviction in my voice.

And you know this because he told you? Connor asks. How the hell would he even know? Just because he's fine now, doesn't mean he'll be fine tomorrow. Don't you get it? No one even knows how this thing spreads.

I glare at my brother who is trying to be the voice of reason, and my head spins, disoriented by the sudden reversal of our relationship as much as anything else.

Look, I say, I trust him.

But then I wonder, if that's true, wouldn't he still be here?

And I remember what that booklet said. It isn't about knowing your partners, it's about a disease that doesn't care if he's a good guy who loves his little sister.

Connor sighs and looks for someplace to sit. Choosing a blue patterned chair we didn't have the last time he was here, he says, Michael, I'm not saying he's a jerk or anything. But that doesn't change the fact that he's been putting himself out there. We all have. Stop thinking with your dick for ten minutes and find someone else.

Like you're one to talk, I throw back.

For a minute he looks hurt, and I know I've gone too far. Connor, I ask finally, dreading his answer. Are you okay?

My brother holds my eyes for a minute. *Answer me*, I think. But he doesn't, he just throws me a bottle of pills.

What is this? I ask.

Antibiotics, he says. Someone told me they might help fend off an infection. Or help if you have one. Or something.

The bottle is unmarked, and I'm too afraid to ask where he got them. I throw it back and say, It doesn't matter. Gabriel and I didn't have sex, and I don't know if I'm even going to see him again.

Connor's shoulders relax, and he allows himself a moment to look relieved. Then he tosses the pills back to me again.

Keep them, he says, back to his usual attitude. I'm sure you're going to pop your cherry at some point.

I don't exactly throw Connor out; but I assist him in finding the door.

But then, in the silence, it hits me.

Connor is right. Gabriel might be sick and not even know it.

Connor might be sick and not telling me.

220

I don't know how to protect them.

I don't know how to protect myself.

How do I live my life without becoming a statistic?

My parents return. My dad grumbles about the traffic and the prices and my mom taking too long to pack.

My mom looks at me, but doesn't really see me. She tells me not to forget to take out the trash.

I fantasize about standing in the middle of the living room and screaming that I've had my heart broken, but I doubt anyone would care.

I call Becky and offer to meet her at St. Patrick's when she gets off work. I don't need to bribe her to hang out with me. I actually want to go to the church and lose myself in the quiet. And maybe she'll have some insights for me.

After I meet her and hug her and basically can't form words for over a half hour, she leads me to a pew.

It'll feel better after you talk about it, she says.

I'm skeptical about that, but it's Becky so I tell her everything.

She takes my hand in hers and says, Okay, first off, I don't know anything about what Connor gave you, but Andy's mom always talks about how there is no cure or prevention for this thing, so promise me you're going to ignore those pills. Seriously, Michael.

And I know you think Connor can be a bit self-absorbed,

but taking the risk to come to your apartment is probably the nicest thing I've heard of him doing.

Yes on both counts, I say.

But as for Gabriel...

Don't judge him, Becks, I beg, I'm not sure I have the energy.

I feel her hand tense in mine, but all she says is, I'm not judging. He's old enough to make up his own mind about how to live his life. And I give him credit for being honest with you. But don't hate me for being glad you didn't sleep with him.

I know I should be glad too, but I'm not, I mumble. Not if I'm being really honest.

Oh, Michael, she says as she puts her arm around me and pulls me close. Do you know what I repeat to myself when I wake up in the middle of the night and Mom is gone or puking in the bathroom?

What?

This too shall pass, she says. Seriously, I get that it sounds sappy, but sometimes that's the only thing that gets me through the day, just being aware that the time will come when I look back on this and know how it all plays out. Even if that sucks.

But what do I do in the meantime? I ask.

The bells start to ring, but somehow I can still hear her whisper one word: live.

I'm sleepwalking.

James calls one day to check up on me, Becky the next.

My mom tries to feed me and my dad glares at me as if I'm in a shitty mood for no other reason than to annoy him.

So really, life as usual.

Except this time, Connor gives *me* a hard time when I cancel dinner. Go figure.

I'm dimly aware of the phone ringing in the middle of the night. My sleep-addled brain says Gabriel, but I haven't called him and I don't think he'd call me.

And definitely not in the middle of the night.

I ignore it because I'm sure it's a wrong number, or a prank, or one of those calls saying a distant relative has died. Besides, I don't have a phone in my room, and I have no plans of getting up.

But the minute my mother opens my bedroom door without knocking, I know it's something else.

Becky's on the line, she whispers.

Becky? I repeat. I glance at the clock. One thirty in the morning. My mother stands still, silent. Everything she has to say is written in her expression. She's the one who will have to deal with my father's annoyance at being woken in the middle of the night, but she doesn't even look put out.

I bolt out of bed, into the kitchen, and grab the phone.

Becks?

Michael. Her fear, her panic, is clear in the tight pitch of her voice.

What is it?

It's James, she says. Andy called. It's pure luck that they were there. His patrol, I mean.

James? Becks, what happened?

I don't know, she says and can't hold the sob in anymore. He was outside The Space. I think he was hurt pretty badly.

I can't process what she's saying. Hurt? James? What does that mean? A broken ankle? Was he hit by a bus?

Becks?

Andy is coming to pick me up. If we wait near the first car of the 1 at Times Square for you, will your parents let you come to St. Vincent's with us?

He's in the hospital? I'm not even asking my parents.

I just go.

This is what Andy tells me:

It was luck, stupid luck that we were even there on patrol. And I didn't see what happened. I just saw him lying there on the ground next to the back door. There was blood. Man, there was so much blood. My patrol leader, Radar, tried to get him to talk while I called 911. James kept mumbling that he was sorry. But I couldn't get him to tell me what he was sorry for, and then he blacked out when the ambulance got there.

Hey Michael, are you sure you want to hear this? You look kind of green.

We aren't relatives, so we can't see him while he's still in the ER.

Over and over the nurses tell us this as if we didn't know, couldn't read their stupid signs.

His parents aren't here. He isn't close to them. Has anyone even called them?

It doesn't matter that we love him. It doesn't matter that he loves us.

We aren't relatives.

Andy doesn't say anything about being worried to have cleaned up James's blood, which I'm taking as a good sign, but I'm not sure what of.

He goes back on patrol while Becky scrounges for change for the cigarette machine and eventually borrows two quarters and a menthol from the duty nurse.

We head out to the loading dock so I can find some air.

Maybe we can break into his room, she says. If we got in, do you think they'd believe we're related?

I stare at Becky's long straight braid, picture my curly hair, and think of James and his blond bangs and his sky-blue eyes and his straight lines, and try to laugh. But it comes out like a strangled cough.

What if it's bad, Becks? What are we going to do? I ask. I selfishly realize I'm as worried about us as I am about James. It isn't that I can't stand the idea of losing anything or anyone else, it's that James is the person my mind goes to when things are dark. He's like this comforting light I need to know is out there somewhere. My brain refuses to contemplate how dim my life would be without him.

She takes my hand, and says, Maybe we should go home. I left his mom a message and she won't be able to reach me so easily here. I jump off the dock and then give her a hand. I don't want to leave. Home seems too far away. But she's right.

Becky calls later and tells me James's mom called her from England and is on her way back. Then she says she talked to Andy's mom who convinced the duty nurse to promise to let her know when James is going to be released, so there's nothing to do but wait.

In the meantime, I try to reach my brother.

There's no answer at the apartment, regardless of when I call.

There's no answer when I go there and pound on the door.

He isn't at work, but I leave a note telling him to call me or I'll throw the entire baseball card collection that Grandpa Bartolomeo left him down the incinerator.

That does the trick.

I miss Gabriel, but it's more like I miss the possibility of Gabriel. With James, it's different, tangible. I keep imagining him, pale against the white sheets, alone and scared.

Connor pulls the celery out of his Bloody Mary and pretends to play the drums with it. James will be okay, he says. I mean, you guys are tight. He knows you're there for him.

I look up at my brother, amazed at his sincerity. Then he says, Hey, wanna hear some good news?

I freeze with a fry in my hand and Connor's words ringing in my ears. Still, I'm not sure I actually believe them.

Give me that again, I say.

A big smile creeps across his face and he repeats, Well, that designer, Maurice, came into the store last month, and we started talking about fashion trends and you know, other stuff, and then we kinda started spending time together. He's into clean living and all of that. Not even pot, just a glass of wine on occasion. How wild is that?

Anyhow, his designs are doing really well, and my friend Brandon is coming back to New York and needs me out of his apartment, so I had to find something anyhow, and we decided it last night. I'm moving in.

With Maurice the shoe guy?

Yeah.

You don't feel like you're maybe rushing it or something?

Life is short, Michael. Seriously, you should see this place. Also, Maurice is hot. And talented and not only as a designer, if you catch my drift. So what the hell? I mean, I've been spending all my nights there anyhow.

Well, that explains why you haven't been returning my calls, I grumble. I thought you were really sick again or something.

Instead of confirming or denying the point, he stares at me with a goofy grin on his face. So even though I think he's being ridiculous, and even though living with someone doesn't mean he won't be doing drugs or having sex with a million people, it seems like a start.

But look, he says, I want you to meet him.

I wait for him to follow his words with something snarky, but nothing comes, so I lean over and put my hand on his forehead like Mom used to do when we were kids.

You're feverish, right? I ask, even though his skin is cool.

My brother has never gone out of his way to introduce me to anyone before. Not even Tony who was apparently worth getting kicked out of the house for.

Connor doesn't even bat my hand away; he just grins wider and says, I'm not. At least I don't think I am. My glands are still a little sore, but I went to the doctor last week, and they can't find anything. Go figure. But anyway, the store is having its annual open house next week. Let's all meet up.

I stare at my brother, wide-eyed. Trying to process everything he's told me.

Then I tell him I'll be there. There's no way I'm missing this.

I get in to see James for ten minutes before he's released. His arm is in a sling. His face is a mass of bruises. Stitches crisscross his swollen lips. I wonder what the club kids or those newspaper writers who are always talking about his cheekbones would think if they saw him now. If they saw him damaged and discolored.

His eyes aren't quite focused, and it disturbs me in a way that must show on my face. It's the medications, the nurse explains.

I bend down so I'm level with the wheelchair they're insisting he use.

You scared us, I say.

James puts a long shaky hand to his chest. I can't feel it, he says. His voice is equally shaky and not quite James.

Feel what?

My heart beating.

I know this is the drugs too, but my eyes sting with sudden tears and my own heart seizes in my rib cage.

I grab his hand and pull it away from his chest. His skin is cold, and his bare fingers twist with mine.

Do what the doctors tell you, I say stupidly. Call me as soon as you can.

Then he's wheeled away to the waiting car, and I'm left with all of the important things I should have said.

All the things I should have asked.

All the things.

Becky gets more details from Andy, who gets the info from his cop dad, who got it from some guy at the precinct who owed him a favor.

And thing is, it was random. Just a bunch of assholes looking for trouble and finding my best friend instead.

I close my eyes and see it. The show is over. James is outside, still in his stage makeup, or maybe dressed to go out. Smoking a long, thin cigarette in his long, thin hand when a guy comes up to him. Then more than one. Maybe they had a tire iron or a baseball bat or maybe just fists.

It could have been anyone. Someone. No one. But they were there. And James, who never has issues with anyone because he isn't a fighter. He can't talk his way out of this one.

Charm can't cut through hate. Anger. Fear.

I wince with each hit I imagine. Eyes. Nose. Mouth.

James.

Broken.

Becky is at Andy's and then heading to work. Connor is at Maurice's. It doesn't matter where my parents are, because what type of comfort have they given me in the last two years?

I caress my guitar. I write James a song. No, a melody. I can't sort through my brain to find words.

I clean my room, alphabetizing my albums and packing away old comics I haven't read in years.

I migrate to the kitchen, pick up the phone to call Gabriel, and then put it back down.

Pick it up again. Punch in numbers. The Dial-a-Daze line gives me a busy signal over and over.

I spend hours staring out of my window at the traffic, wondering what happens next.

Becky calls from the ice cream store.

My boss is off tonight, come down and keep me company, she says.

I don't know, Becks…

Michael, did that sound like a question? I'm freezing my ass off in here, and I just served fudge ripple to an entire little league team.

Fine, I say, fine.

I bring her my Clash sweatshirt to put on under her apron, and I can't stop thinking that it was the same one James wore at my house. She pushes me onto a stool and instructs me to sit and watch while she scoops some daiquiri ice into the blender, followed by something clear she dumps in from a brown paper bag.

When the machine shuts off, she pours two cups and holds one out to me.

You look like you could use it.

You haven't heard from James yet? I ask after a couple of mind-numbingly cold sips.

Seriously, Michael. He isn't going to call *me*.

I thought you might have tried to reach him.

Well, I did. But of course his parents have that stupid answering machine. Seriously. I wasn't just going to leave a message again, regardless of how eloquently his mother asked for it. I mean, it's saved on tape. *Forever*. And who knows who could be listening in.

I stay at the store until ten, listening to the tinny sixties music coming over the speakers and drinking daiquiri slush.

No one else comes in until just before I leave. Then I'm surprised to see Andy show up wearing his full vigilante getup—red cap and all.

Sorry about James, man, he says. I'm glad we got there in time. You know, otherwise it might have been worse.

Worse. The word makes the freezing liquid climb up the back of my throat.

I know it happens. But I don't get why anyone would do that? I croak out.

It's a sport to these guys, Andy says. They go looking for f— Sorry, for guys who are obviously gay.

But seriously, I say, James wouldn't hurt a fly.

Andy shakes his head and says, Welcome to New York City, Michael. When did that ever matter here?

Connor and Maurice stand at one of the tall tables that have been set up around the store. They're looking at each other like they're the only ones in the room.

Maurice is tall. Has dark close-shaved hair, super-intense eyes, and a faint trace of some sort of Midwestern accent. And yeah, Connor is right. He's hot. And nice, actually. Like genuinely nice and not the least bit condescending when he asks about school and my music. He listens politely when I answer his questions, and he talks about his fashion stuff as if he hasn't had to answer the same questions twenty times tonight alone.

Next to him, Connor is glowing in a way I haven't seen before. He's relaxed, and I try to remember a time, even when we were kids, when he seemed so comfortable in his skin; like maybe he doesn't feel as if he needs to prove himself twenty-four-seven. He gets us all a round of soda (seriously, my brother is drinking soda!) and leans toward Maurice whenever he speaks.

I owe Connor for the hundred million times he's embarrassed me in front of someone, but I can't bring myself to reciprocate. And when Maurice is pulled away to talk to some reporter, Connor actually looks nervous when he asks, So?

I like him, I say honestly. Then, because we're still brothers and Connor is still Connor, I add, I mean, not sure what he's doing with you, but...

Surprisingly, Connor's expression goes serious. I know, he says, rubbing the back of his neck, I know. I've fucked up so many things, but this feels like it's all been worth it. Even getting kicked out.

I watch his eyes search the room and then brighten when they land on Maurice. Then he says, I hope I don't screw this up.

Seriously, what planet am I on?

James finally calls. I think I'm in hell, he says. Meanwhile, I think it's heaven to hear his voice.

James's parents' house in Connecticut has columns, water views, landscaped gardens. Is it really so bad? I ask.

He pauses and the line crackles when he answers, It's Dante's ninth circle, Michael.

Which circle is that? I ask. We don't get to Dante until next year.

He breathes out one word that makes the hair stand up on the back of my neck: treachery.

I really need a cigarette, he says after pause.

I ask, Do you want me to send you some? Cigarettes are almost a dollar a pack now, and I have no idea how much postage would cost, but I'd do it if he asked.

Thanks, he says. I'll sort something out.

There's another pause. An odd uncomfortable silence that

233

demands to be filled with the question I don't know how to ask, but need to.

Are you okay?

James makes a sound that's something like a sigh, then says, Let's just say I'm not spending a lot of time looking in the mirror. Lord, I hope those doctors took sewing in school. I'd hate to think the only roles I'm ever going to get are as Frankenstein's monster.

I'm glad to hear him joking, but there's no trace of the smile I expect to hear in his voice.

What did the police say? I ask, although I know from Andy they have no suspects.

Oh, Michael, seriously? What do you think they said? That it was random. Wrong place, wrong time. That sort of thing. But even if they'd caught someone, you know how these things play out. They'll claim I made a pass as them, that they simply couldn't help but protect themselves from the onslaught of my passions. As if.

Anyhow, he continues, I'm getting a lot a reading done. And all of my old albums are here, and Mother's doctor is loose with the pain killers, so it could be worse.

Without James, the city is duller.

With so little time before school starts, I feel like even trying to make something of the remaining days is pointless.

I don't know what I did with myself before I started hanging out at The Echo, so I have no idea how to fill the time now. Becky got Andy to commit to taking a night off patrol and seeing her on Friday nights. Connor is spending all of his time with Maurice.

And I'm alone.

I think about calling Gabriel, but even if I reached him, I don't know what I'd say. Every place I want to go holds the possibility of seeing him, and while that's what I want most, it's probably what I need least. Not like anything is going to be any different.

And not like he's called me.

So instead, I play my guitar. I hang out on the fire escape and people-watch. I stare at the clock until the nights end.

I meet up with Becky and fill her in on my talk with James. When I'm done talking, she fumbles in her bag and hands me a roll of quarters.

What are these for?

She grabs my arm and says, Video arcade.

This always helps when I'm hurt or pissed off, she says and shoots another centipede.

Becky's making minimum, $3.35 an hour, so we're quickly running through three hours of her scooping ice cream at work.

But then it's my turn, and I realize that over the din of the machines and the clanking of the coins and the constant talking, you can't hear the sirens outside, and I can't really hold onto thoughts of losing Gabriel or missing James, and my brain is only focused on the roller ball and blasting this stupid bug into oblivion.

We stop at the door of Howard Johnson's.

I don't know if I want to go in without James here, Becky says. Is that strange?

No, I was just thinking the same thing.

We grab slices of pizza at the Ray's down the block instead, but one bite is all I can handle.

I don't know what to do, I admit. I can't even go to The Echo. Plus, I feel like I'm stuck lying to my parents until I move out or die.

I've been thinking about that, she says. I told my mom last night that if she doesn't clean up, I'm going to leave and move in with Andy's family or something. I was worried I couldn't tell his parents anything with his dad being a cop and all, but I talked to his mom and they're going to try to get mine some help. Anyhow, I think that's maybe an option. Of course, I'd rather my mom clean her life up… Then I thought we could make a pact, and you could talk to your parents too. I mean, if you were going to anyhow.

Reasons to come out to my parents:
→ *Solidarity with Becky*
→ *Be true to myself*
→ *Make Connor feel like he isn't alone*
→ *Piss off my dad*
→ *…*

Good that can come from it:
→ *Hell if I know*

Senior year begins, and James still isn't back.

Instead, he calls to tell me his mother wants him to stay in Connecticut where it's "safer." His father, back from a photo shoot in Australia to, James says, "make sure I have my head screwed on correctly," wants him to come to some sort of awards ceremony in DC, hosted by President Reagan.

Maybe it's because I know James so well. Or maybe it's because his anger is so close to the surface, but even on the phone, I can hear it welling up inside him and threatening to spill over. The acid in his voice as he gave a speech in *Blood Makes Noise* about having to stay silent at home rather than argue about the mocking government nonresponse to AIDS in order to keep the peace.

Of course, there's no way I would go, he says. Can you imagine? Being in the room with President Reagan and my father at the same time? I think I'd burst into flames. Anyhow, I'll figure something out. I just want to get back to the city.

On a whim, I call a little club in the East Village that's doing open mics on Tuesday nights, the same nights they do buy-one-get-two on drinks. You never know if the audience is going to love everything because they're drunk or hate everything for the same reason.

I tell them I'm interested in being added to the list, but I lie about my age and lie about my phone number.

Then I hang up when I realize I was lying about my interest.

It's too early in the year for serious homework, and I'm feeling lost, so I head to Vinnie's Videos. I don't even feel like watching a movie, but I need to do *something*.

I search through the comedies, knowing that nothing is going to make me laugh.

Bartolomeo, someone calls.

I turn to see Adam Rose, this guy from school, his blue work apron eclipsed by the massive stack of videos he's supposed to be re-shelving. Hold on, he says.

He sets the stack down, all but one copy of *Tron*. Seriously, he says, pointing to a label on the tape's front that reads PLEASE BE KIND; REWIND. How hard is it to rewind a freaking tape before you return it?

I shrug.

So, what are you looking for? Need a recommendation or anything?

I scan the shelves. Do you have any movies to watch when you really aren't in the mood to watch a movie, but you need to stop thinking for a while? I ask.

I'm not sure why I've spewed all that. Adam and I have had some classes together, but it isn't like we really hang out. He's part of the music clique, though, so maybe in another life, we could have been friends.

He glances at the clock and says, If you don't want to watch anything, you're welcome to tag along with me. I'm going to a party at David Hayne's place when I get off. His parents are out of town.

A party sounds like something that will take more energy than I have. But then I look around at the store. At the torn video cases and the too-bright lights. At some little kid whose parents are dragging him out of the store for screaming about wanting to play *Donkey Kong*.

Sure, I say, surprising both of us.

Not like I have anything else to do.

I go home, change, and throw some mousse in my hair. Then I meet Adam back at the store. Normally quiet, he tries to entertain me with stories from the video store and doesn't seem to mind when I nod back distractedly.

We bus it crosstown to the Upper East Side and the Haynes' apartment building. Adam presses the button, and we're buzzed in. I can hear the music as soon as we're through the lobby door, The Police singing "Every Breath You Take," which I'm already sick of because it's been playing on every radio station in the city for months.

Adam makes the rounds, saying hello to kids I recognize from school and others I don't think I've seen before. I hate feeling like I don't belong, so I hang back and grab a beer from the cooler.

Across the room, someone opens a box of glow sticks and snaps them to life. Someone else turns out the lights, and people start throwing the gel around so it covers the walls. All I can think is that my parents would kill me if that happened at home. Not even Connor was stupid enough to throw parties in our apartment.

In the eerie light, I start looking through the bookcases. You can tell a lot about people by what they read and listen to, and while I'm not particularly intrigued in the private interests of the Haynes family, it at least makes me look as though I'm doing something.

Have you read that? I turn to see a boy pointing at a book. The spine says, *Brideshead Revisited.*

I shake my head and say, No, but my friend James kept trying to get me to watch the BBC version. He was obsessed.

You should give it a try, he says. The boy has dusky skin and a cute, timeless look. Black eyes and dark short hair. No eyeliner. No club clothes. No effort.

He tells me he's eighteen, his name is River, and he's David's cousin, visiting from Amherst for the week.

I stare at him, thinking of David's blond curls.

My mom is Black, he says as if he can read my mind. I wonder how many times he's been asked about it tonight. My dad and Dave's dad are brothers. He's using me as the excuse for this party, but it really isn't my thing.

He smiles easily, and I find myself smiling back, slightly overwhelmed by the amount of information he's just thrown at me. Parties aren't my thing either, I confess.

The music changes and catches my attention. My confusion must be obvious because River says, Talking Heads, "Psycho Killer," I have no idea what it's about, but it's pretty cool. Very New York.

I sometimes wonder about the New York that only exists in the minds of tourists.

I have this whole album on cassette if you want to hear it, River says, gesturing down a hallway at a closed door.

He looks at me expectantly, and I feel a flash of attraction and curiosity. I don't usually assume that any boy who talks to me about books and music is hitting on me, but something about this boy is different. Or maybe I'm different. Maybe it doesn't even matter.

Maybe it's simply time for me to stop waiting for everyone else to tell me what to do. Or what not to do. Maybe it's time to just be myself.

River smiles, and before I can chicken out, I channel my brother, say, Lead the way, and follow River to the guest room.

The room looks like a holding tank for 1975. Shag carpet, lava lamps, even a beaded curtain.

I look around while River moves a brown furry pillow to uncover a Walkman. He takes the cassette out and puts it into a boom box on the dresser, the only thing here that belongs in this decade.

I tell him I play guitar. I tell him there's a dance club I like. I tell him where I live and what classes I took last year and where I like to go to eat.

I ask him what he's done in New York and what he does in Massachusetts, and we talk about music and art, and how he's been homeschooled and is looking forward to going to college.

He tells me he's leaving in the morning. Going back to Amherst and then heading to Europe to go hiking for an entire year before he starts at Berkeley.

That sounds nice, I say, which must be the beer talking because the idea of slogging through the forest for a year sounds awful to me. Maybe I'll do something like that if my parents kick me out.

Why would they kick you out? he asks.

I consider making something up, but I'll probably never see him again and that makes me bold. My father kicked my brother out when they found out he was gay, I say, waiting to hear his reaction.

That sucks, he says and swallows loudly. He gets up and forwards the tape to the song he says is his favorite. The singer starts singing about wanting to be home and already being there. *Lucky him.*

And you're worried they'll do the same to you? River asks, not looking at me.

I take a deep breath and say, My father hasn't exactly mellowed since.

River turns, his face illuminated by the pink of the lava lamp. I got lucky in the parent department, he says. Mine are ex-hippies. They actually met in a commune, if you can believe it. There are pictures of my sister and me at Woodstock. Anyhow, my parents believe in free love and all that. They think we've become a repressed society.

I feel the tension leave my body in one gush. My father thinks AIDS is nature's way of punishing us, I say.

We both laugh the way people do when something isn't at all funny. He stops first and takes a step toward me, his face getting serious. I'm sorry, River says. I'm sorry that you have to deal with that.

He reaches out his hand and puts it on my arm. Is this okay? he asks, moving his fingers down to grasp mine.

His voice is soft, concerned. He smells like Polo. His fingers are calloused, and the roughness of them against my skin makes me flush.

I wait for my head to fill with warnings: Don't be stupid, Michael. You aren't the type to mess around with a boy at a party; you're still hooked on Gabriel. But Gabriel isn't here and my head is quiet. My body on the other hand is a mass of sensation, everything shaking, spinning, throbbing.

I'm going back to Boston tomorrow, River continues, but his voice sounds like it's coming from somewhere far away. I'm not trying to be presumptuous, he says, but I can't get involved or anything.

The whole year seems to hit me all at once, just as the lava lamp sends swirls of pink and purple over River's elegant face.

I'm not my brother. I'd never want to be so *out there*. But maybe Connor isn't the only one allowed to do something simply because it feels good once in a while.

And more than anything, this feels good. River has moved, and he's standing so close to me I can feel him pressed against me in a million different places, and I know I should be nervous and I am, but it's like I can't really feel *that*. All I feel is River. All I want to feel is him.

Then he steps back, and I feel a strange sort of cold, of hunger, and I place my hand flat on his chest.

Michael, he breathes out, and I know, somehow, that I could walk away now and he'd still be cool, and I know that I'd be an idiot not to be afraid. But I still don't believe that hiding from the world is the way to deal with anything. Not for me, anyhow.

I take a deep breath and walk over and lock the door.

Everything about River is relaxed. He's considerate and confident and sexy as hell. And it's almost like he's memorized the pamphlet in Connor's old apartment, because while we do a lot of the things I read about and imagined trying with Gabriel, he's got condoms and follows all the other safety ideas it suggested.

He doesn't do anything to point out how inexperienced I am. And because I know I'm unlikely to see him again, I'm less inhibited than I was with Gabriel. It's easy to touch him. Easy to let him touch me.

When he tells me, after, that he'd be happy if I spent the night and crashed with him, it's easy to say yes.

But none of that keeps thoughts of my missed chances with Gabriel out of my head, and I barely get any sleep.

In the morning, River asks me for my address so he can send me postcards from Europe.

Filled with guilt over my thoughts of Gabriel, I panic and give him Becky's address instead.

I stumble out of the apartment, Polo on my skin, dizzy with sex and the realization that my parents are going to kill me for staying out all night without even calling.

The sun is burning down hot for September and reflecting off the pavement as I walk crosstown, so I take my shirt off and tie it around my waist.

I pass early morning joggers in the park and smile at the idea that they can see the shadow of River's mouth on my skin.

I've had sex. Sex with a boy, and I liked it, so hey world, here I am.

I stop at the pay phone on the corner of my block that sometimes gives free calls and punch in the number for Dial-a-Daze.

This number is disconnected, the recording says.

I hold my breath for a minute, but what washes over me is relief. I guess I have to make my own future now.

What do you have to say for yourself?

I'm not sure what wakes me, my father's booming voice or the sunlight that clobbers me in the face when he pulls open my curtain.

At the moment, not much, I mumble.

He rips the comforter off my bed. I'm surprised, given that he did the same thing to Connor once, and my brother, probably still drunk from the night before, punched him in the face.

I roll over and shade my eyes. Dad, seriously, I say. I'm sorry I didn't call.

In truth, I'm not sorry. In truth my entire body is still buzzing, and once I sleep off the fact that I was awake all night, I'm looking forward to figuring out what this all means. How it's changed me.

Because I'm sure it must have. I hope so, anyhow.

My father's face doesn't relax, which comes as no surprise.

Where the hell were you? he asks. Is this how I raised you? Your mother was frantic.

I interrupt him and say, I was at David Hayne's on 86th. He had a party and…

Here, I'm forced to think quickly. What is going to piss him off the least? I go for the most frat boy of options and say, I had a couple of beers and crashed. I know it was stupid. I won't do it again.

A voice in my head says, Tell him. I'm not sure he can really kick me out because, unlike Connor, I'm under eighteen.

I'm tired of hiding, even if it's just from my father.

I'm tired of being dismissed, even if it's just by my father.

And now I need to figure out what to do about it. Even if it just means confronting my father.

I open my mouth, but then my father snorts and walks out of the room.

My shoulders relax. I might have missed an opportunity to take a stand, but at least I've survived to fight another day with a roof over my head.

That night, I pop one of Connor's antibiotics, even though I believe Becky when she tells me that Andy's mom says they won't do anything to fend off getting sick, and stand in front of the full-length mirror in the bathroom, examining my skin. The birthmark on my ankle. The scar on my arm from an unfortunate run-in with Connor's G.I. Joe figure when I was five.

I crane my neck to look at my back.

This is me. This is my baseline. This is what everything in that pamphlet on Connor's counter is trying to protect.

I sit next to Becky in the park, but decide not to tell her about River yet. For a little while, I want what happened to belong to me alone.

I went to *shul* yesterday, she says, for Yom Kippur. You know, you're supposed to spend the day repenting for everything you've done wrong over the past year, but I did a lot of thinking and made a decision. A couple of them, actually.

With Becky, it's hard to tell if that means she's decided what she's getting for lunch, decided what her next sewing project will be, or decided she's moving across the country to grow kumquats. I know better than to react until I know what direction she's heading.

I'm going to make it work with Andy. Somehow. Neither of us wants to be with anyone else, and I don't want to be the girl that bails when things get hard.

I nod. Happy for her, I guess.

And, she says, I'm going to work my ass off at school this year. I'm finally going to be editor of the *Spirit*, and I want the articles in there to matter. I know people want to read about the sports teams and everything, but I feel like there's an opportunity to make some sort of a difference. As much as you can make in a high school paper, anyhow.

I nod in agreement and not only because she looks so happy. There's no reason the school paper can't cover things that are going on outside of our walls.

Then she says, Maybe I'll even convince you to write something.

Me? What would I write about?

The smile that makes its way across her face tells me she's already thought this through and has been waiting for the right moment to hit me with it.

Can you maybe write something about the Gay Pride Parade? she asks. I think it's about time more kids know that they have options.

Why me?

She reaches over and puts a hand flat on my chest. Because you care, Michael, she says. And look at what happened to James. I'm sick of it.

I wince and ramble, I don't know, Becks. I was only there for a couple hours, and I'm still trying to make sense of everything. I'm not sure I'm ready to come out to the whole school.

You can write the article anonymously if you need to. I'm not asking you to do anything you don't feel safe doing.

I don't know. Can I think about it?

She smiles and gives me a hug. Of course you can. Just let me know.

The next Friday, I wake in the middle of the night to the smell of smoke on the fire escape.

Once I realize the building isn't on fire and I'm not dreaming, I rush to the window and climb out.

James, you're back. I throw my arms around him and feel him wince, so I let go and look at him. He looks thinner if possible, and the black angled shirt he's wearing—the one with all the snaps and buckles—hangs loose on him.

My eyes stray to the yellowed bruises on his face. I don't know what to say to a friend who has been beaten, so I stay quiet.

I wasn't sure if I really wanted to wake you, he says. I'm tired as a ghost. I never sleep well at my parents'.

Do you want to come in? I could set an alarm if you want some sleep.

James shakes his head and takes a drag of his cigarette. No, I'm on my way to the apartment, but I wanted to see you. Well, you and Becky, but I can hardly trek out to Queens at this time of night.

She's going to be so glad to see you, I say, already excited for the three of us to catch up.

He stares at the lit end of his cigarette and says, It's going to be a while before that happens, I'm afraid. My parents have decided to send me abroad. Apparently, my father was less than amused when he found out I wasn't actually registered in school. My flight is tomorrow.

Something inside me goes cold. Wait. I croak out. What? You aren't going to go, are you?

James shrugs and looks away.

I'm too tired to fight, he says, and I can hear the truth of his words in his voice. Besides, my father is going to be hanging around for a while, and I'd prefer not to be there as well.

James, you can't leave, I say. Please don't go.

This at least brings a smile to his face. He stares at me, all blue eyes and straight lines and something inside me feels as though it's breaking.

He turns away, eyes landing on the street below. You know, he says, we never really talked about what happened that night after we went to the club.

James, we don't need to…

I just wanted to say that Becky isn't totally off base. There have been times when I've wondered if you and I should…you know… But your friendship means too much to me to risk. Is that odd?

I rub my eyes, feeling like the world has shifted on its axis.

James sighs and leans his head back onto the rail of the stairs, his eyes toward the moon. Don't worry, I'm not hitting on you, he says. It's a moot point, anyhow. I can't imagine being with anyone now or… Oh, Michael, I'm just feeling so lonely and old and maudlin.

"Maudlin" is such a James word that it almost makes me laugh. Anyone else *would* sound a hundred years old if they wanted to use it.

I look at him, weighing my choices. The strangest thing is that I *do* understand what he's saying about not risking our friendship. And even though things ended so badly, I've come to realize that the way I feel about James and the way I felt… feel…about Gabriel, or even River, are very, very different.

I get it, I say, leaning my shoulder into his. But I wish there was something I could do.

James smiles slightly and then the reality of what he said about leaving slaps me in the face.

Where are they sending you? For how long? I ask, but there's no good answer. All I want is for James to tell me I misunderstood.

He takes a long drag on his cigarette. London, he says in a monotone. To my aunt Millie's.

But the show and the apartment and… I let my words fade off, because really, I mean me. What happens to *me* without Gabriel *and* without James?

I'm not sure I could go onstage like this, anyhow, he says and looks away again. I don't know if he means because he's all bruised or because of something else.

But you're the star, I say.

A show is never about a single person, he replies predictably, and they've been managing without me quite well apparently.

I wrack my brain for anything that might make James stay, but before I can put up a fight, he changes the subject and asks: Have you ever held someone's hand while they've died?

I shake my head in the darkness, wondering where this conversation is going and why.

I have, James says. In the last months before I went to my parents, I held the hands of two dying acquaintances and one man I met in the hospital who simply had no one else. I couldn't be there for Steven, so… I'm tired of it, Michael. It's just begun, and I'm already so tired.

He rubs his eyes with his long fingers and says, I don't want to spend all my time worrying about death. Lord, I'm only eighteen.

Aren't people dying in London too? I want to ask. *Can't you stay here?* But really, my heart is pounding, selfishly repeating, *But what about me?* over and over and over.

So instead of saying anything, I take James's hand and squeeze, and we sit like that until the sun rises.

The first thing I do the next day is to look out on the fire escape for cigarette butts, the only sign I have that James was actually here. Instead, I find a note saying he'll write to me, and a sealed letter for me to pass along to Becky.

I race to the kitchen and call the apartment, but when Rob answers, he tells me James has already left for the airport.

Filled with nervous energy, I clean my room, finally packing away the final pieces of my junior year before leaving to meet up with Connor. He's spent the last few weeks with Maurice on Fire Island, so when he meets me in a Wham CHOOSE LIFE T-shirt and blue aviator sunglasses, he's tanned and relaxed and looks like he's walked off the set of a music video.

You're still happy? I ask, even though the answer is obvious.

Life, he says, eyes shining, is a bowl of cherries.

Next to him, dressed in my black club clothes, I look like depression personified, but its Echo, and blending in with the scenery doesn't sound half bad, even if I feel like I have to be here to reclaim part of my life.

We cut through the line waiting in front of the club, and Brian waves us in. Well, he says, if it isn't the return of the prodigal son.

Connor laughs and says, Nah, you obviously haven't met our father. He'd happily sell us both to Satan for a loaf of bread. Well, *me* anyhow.

Echo is the same as the last time I was here. The bar is still sticky. Martin is still trying to solicit beer for his parrot. The music is still teeth-clenchingly loud.

But it's like going back to your old elementary school to visit your teachers and finding the water fountains too low to reach. Maybe The Echo hasn't changed, but I have.

Connor and I dance, and, for once, it isn't his eyes straying around the room, it's mine.

But it doesn't matter where I look. Gabriel isn't here.

Afterward at the diner, Connor gives me the lecture that he's been holding onto all night. A summation of the reasons why I'm better off without Gabriel, all the reasons why I'd be safer, happier, and more interesting, if I could forget about him.

I'm glad my brother cares, but I don't really give a shit about his opinion on this.

Just because you're finally happy doesn't make you Dr. Ruth, I say. Although the thought of Connor as a fifty-something radio sex therapist is surprisingly amusing.

And just because you've had a one-night stand, doesn't make you Rob Lowe, he replies.

Dear Michael:

London is suffering me about as well as I'm suffering it. At least Big Ben hasn't stopped ringing (You do realise that Ben is the bell and not the tower, correct?). And so, life goes on.

Unbeknownst to me, my aunt graciously volunteered my services to a local theatre troupe. They are putting on the most god-forsakenly irrelevant production of My Fair Lady *(well, is there* any such thing as a relevant production of My Fair Lady? One wonders...). Anyhow, you can imagine how difficult it has been to hide my glee at being part of such a piece of artistic merit (insert sarcasm here).

I hope your brother is still over the moon. I hope Becky is behaving herself. Or perhaps not, so long as she's happy. Please give her a hug and tell her to expect a letter as well. As you can imagine, I got quite an earful from her in the post for leaving without seeing her.

I hear what you're saying about writing for the paper. I agree. I'm not sure that's the correct place to work out your feelings, since you're so confused about them, anyhow. Also, I don't think Becky will hate you if you say no. I mean, she's still my friend and I say no to her frequently.

As for Gabriel... Oh, Michael, I'm not sure I know what to tell you. But that you're still thinking about him says something. Someone once told me that things left undone leave more of a wound than things that are done, but which cause pain. I guess that's my way of saying it might be good for you to see him at least once more. Then see how you feel. Maybe, if nothing else, you can end up as friends. Although I suspect you're looking for more than that.

Either way, please get your passport and come visit me in this wilderness. I'm afraid I'm picking up more of an accent than I'd like. You must save me.

I miss you and Becky desperately.

Love, or whatever you need most,
James

The next day, I reread James's letter and plan to write back, telling him I'll get my passport as soon as I can figure out how to without having to ask my parents to sign anything or whenever I have the guts to take Connor up on his offer to forge Dad's signature. But even then, I have no idea when or if I'll find a way to make it to London. I just need him to come back soon.

But first, I pick up my guitar. Try to find the rhythms and pauses in my thoughts. Think about James holding the hand of some dying guy he didn't even know.

Then I play so many minor chords it makes me cry tears I know I haven't earned.

Becky is bummed, but understanding, when I tell her I can't write for her. You'll find a way to tell your story, she says.

But I don't have a story, I respond.

Everyone has a story, Michael. Maybe you just don't know the plot of yours yet.

After he kicked Connor out, after my mom barricaded herself in the bedroom without having stood up for her oldest son, after I watched my brother stumble up the street with his suitcase— all my father let him take—to go who-knows-where, my father burst into my room and told me we were going to talk.

If you have something to say to me, Michael, say it now, he ordered.

I had plenty of things to say, but I wasn't my brother, so I stayed quiet.

Dad and I still hung out a bit back then, and even though he and Connor fought all the time, I usually blamed my brother for egging him on.

I never thought Dad would make good on all his threats. I thought he was going to ask how I felt about him throwing Connor out of the house, until he said, Don't think the same won't happen to you if you ever humiliate me and your mother like that.

And then I thought he was talking about the public method Connor had chosen, until he added, Had I wanted a son-in-law, I would have impregnated your mother with a daughter.

I was twelve. I hadn't said it out loud, but I knew I was gay.

And I knew nothing would ever be the same. I knew enough to stay silent.

I'm tired of staying silent.

Our senior year started off with the same sense of anticipation that every school year brings.

But something about this year feels different. Who can care about memorizing Chaucer in Middle English when so much is going on in the world right now?

When I complain to Becky, I think she gets it because she says: Find some way to make a difference. Volunteer somewhere. Make your voice heard. But stay safe, Michael. Whatever that means, somehow always stay safe.

The fear lab has also changed. There's no paper, just a note from the counseling office with their hours on it and a reminder that anyone caught defacing school property will be suspended.

Now there's no chance for people to share their fears. The walls have been paneled over as if that can erase history. Erase fear.

As if that's fucking possible.

Something inside me snaps. I walk into the library and borrow a marker from the cup on the reference desk.

And on the wall, I write:

My name is Michael Bartolomeo and I'm scared.

Scared I'm never going to be able to look anyone in the eye and admit to being gay.

Scared I'm never going to feel safe showing someone I love them in public.

Scared I'm going to die.

Scared they're all going to convince me to stay silent.

Scared I'm going to let them.

Silence is not the answer.

All day, I wait:

→ *Wait to be called to the office*

→ *Wait to be kicked out of school*

→ *Wait to feel sorry for what I've done, but that doesn't happen*

My brother came out loudly, high as a kite on the stage of our high school.

I'm not sure if my words are quieter or if I want them to be.

I feel light. Unburdened. Like I've finally done something. Or am starting to.

257

Becky pulls me into a janitor's closet that's most commonly used for making out. It smells like bleach and Windex and is probably the least romantic place in the world.

Are you okay? she asks, leaning against a rack of cleaning supplies and looking me up and down.

I'm fine, Becks. Really, I'm good.

So, you're really out now, she says.

Yeah, I guess so.

To the whole school.

Yup.

And you're okay with that?

I wait for the usual knot in my stomach to form, but it doesn't. I am, I say. I mean, I'm sure I'm going to hear about it, but yes, I'm okay with it.

She throws her arms around me and pulls me tight. I'm so, so proud of you, she says. And James will be too. I'm sure of it.

Then, as we part, she takes a roll of paper towel and clubs me lightly over the head with it. We'll talk later about you defacing the library, she says with a smirk. And instead of writing on the wall, you could have just written for the paper and given me an exclusive, you know.

I skip my next two classes and corner my brother at work.

Connor stares at me, unblinking. It isn't like I need him to approve, but I thought I should give him a heads-up before the family shit hits the fan.

He leans back in the chair in his boss's office and crosses his arms. I can almost see the wheels spinning in his head.

Okay, he says. Yeah, okay. Control the situation. Don't make the same mistake I made, not that I made a mistake, but you know what I'm saying. Don't give Dad the upper hand. Be ready for the explosion. Have a plan.

What kind of plan? I ask. I still have a year of school. But this is going to get back to them at some point.

My brother bounces in his seat. I got it, he says. Move in with us. Mo won't mind. We've got the room, and he's going to be in Europe most of the next few months, anyhow.

Mo? I ask, and my brother actually blushes. You can't just invite me to move into someone else's apartment, Connor, I say. But in the back of my mind, it sounds like a damn good idea. At least until James can talk his parents into letting him come home. Maybe we can get a place together or something, then.

It's all good, Connor says. Seriously. Although warning you, I can't cook for shit.

I'm dizzy. It feels like I'm in a taxi going too fast down Broadway and the storefronts and buildings are spinning around too quickly to identify.

What am I doing?

I walk into the office and ask to see the school counselor. It's going to happen anyhow, and I'd rather just face my punishment head-on and get it over with.

Since I've never been in trouble before, Ms. Davis calls it an unfortunate act of impulsivity "given the times." Aside from the mandatory day of suspension, I have to clean and re-stain the wood panel and then check in with her once a week for the next month.

Then she adds that, due to the suspension, she's going to have to notify my parents.

My chest constricts, and I take in a shaky lungful of air. In my head, Connor says, Control the situation.

But really, what does that mean when everything in the world is out of my control?

I ask her to wait until the end of the week to call them and promise to apologize to the library staff. Oddly enough, she agrees.

Talk builds through the halls in a rumble, and I hear my name whispered for days. I spend a lot of time looking over my shoulder, waiting for what happened to James to happen to me. But aside from a couple of under-the-breath comments in the hall, no one bothers me. A few kids even come up and thank me or just smile sadly and then turn away.

Mr. Solomon pulls me aside and sternly tells me I shouldn't have chosen to write on a library wall, but then he softens and says quietly that he's proud of my courage.

I nod, but really all I've done is scribbled some words onto a wall. And I'm not sure how much that means or what it could possibly change.

Surprisingly, it's Adam Rose who spells it out for me when he pulls me aside after a spirit event.

You've got guts, he says. I'll give you that.

I didn't really do anything, I insist.

He's quiet for a minute as the room empties out. Then he says, Do you remember my cousin Paul? He graduated last year.

Paul. Stocky. Baseball player. Catcher, I think. Straight brown hair. I seem to remember him having some issues with drugs that got him kicked off the team.

Yeah, I say. I remember him.

Did you ever meet his dad?

I shake my head.

Adam's eyes go misty and he says, Well, Paul's dad in New York Presbyterian. He's my favorite uncle, and I don't think he's going to make it. I told him what you'd written, and it made him cry. He said he didn't know that anyone our age was even paying attention to what's going on.

A chill goes through me. Being afraid of some enemy you can't see, regardless of how big or deadly, is one thing. Starting to recognize the people lying dead on the battlefield is something else entirely.

Unlike Connor, I don't deliberately out myself to my parents. That task is left to Ms. Davis, who is, I guess, just doing her job.

I find this out when I come home from school on Friday. When my mother, drinking sherry out of a thimble-sized glass, tells me in grim voice, Your father is on his way home.

A list of the immediate casualties caused by my writing sixty-six words into a language lab wall:

→ *One bruise on my arm.*

→ *Fourteen pieces of broken glass from the old Christmas picture over the TV that fell when my father threw a pepper mill at it.*

→ *A hundred of my mother's tears.*

→ *An infinite number of shards from the shattered metaphorical closet door.*

I try to ride out my father's anger and hope that, at his core, he doesn't really want to kick me out.

The next morning, a Saturday, I creep out of my bedroom and approach him while he's eating breakfast.

I didn't do this to piss you off, I say. It's just who I am, and I can't ignore what's going on in the world. People are dying. How can I just stand by and watch?

How could anyone?

My father eats his toast and boiled eggs. He doesn't look up from his food for a very long time.

When he does, he says, I always knew that nothing would come from your brother. But I had hopes for you, Michael, and you're throwing them all away just to spite me. How do you expect me to face my friends? Our neighbors? What is your mother going to say to the women at church? Why couldn't you have just kept your mouth shut?

This has nothing to do with either of you, I reply before I can stop myself.

My father's face goes a familiar shade of red, and I picture how things might have gone down with Gabriel and his father.

I'm bringing a boy home for dinner, Gabriel might have said. Tell him to be here by six, his father might have replied. That scenario will never play out with my family, and I just can't do it anymore. It's completely clear that it isn't about whether I'm having sex or not or who with, it's about needing to breathe. I've never understood my brother more.

So, what? You want me to move out too? I ask my father.

He looks at me, and more calmly than I've ever heard him, in a voice completely devoid of emotion, says, Yes, Michael, I think that might be for the best.

At first I assume Dad will just pretend Connor isn't here. That his older son isn't standing at the door for the first time in years, ready to help his younger son move out.

Wishful thinking at its best.

Instead, before he walks out and slams the door so hard, the pictures slant on the wall, it's: This is your fault, Connor. I knew you were going to drag Michael down into the gutter with you.

The stuff I care about fills a couple of boxes.
- → *Some clothes, tapes, and books.*
- → *A few photographs.*
- → *The star off my ceiling.*
- → *The beads from Pride.*
- → *My guitar.*
That's it.

My mother has gone to church or a friend's or a bar. I have no idea where my father went.

Connor stops at the door to my room. His expression is complicated when he looks around and says, You're sure, right? I'm not telling you that you shouldn't be, just…

As his voice trails off, I glance around the room. At the stuff I'm leaving behind. At the ceiling I've stared at all my life. At the bed where Gabriel and I came so close to having sex.

Then I look back at my brother and see him in a way I never have. At the courage he must have needed to stand tall on that stage and write his own future.

I'm sure, I say, picking up my boxes. I'm sure.

Instead of having dinner with just Connor on Wednesdays, we both meet up with Mom.

Every week, she brings a bag with a little more of my stuff, and I finally feel moved into Maurice and Connor's apartment.

Every week, she grills me about school and asks about Becky and whether I've heard from James. She asks Connor about work and, as an afterthought because my brother keeps bringing him up, about Maurice, and we talk about everything except for my father, because really, what is there to say?

She never apologizes.

Only once do I manage to get her alone and ask why she stays with him.

She hugs me and says, Life looks different from my age than it looks from sixteen, Michael. I've made my bed.

No one expects you to stay in a bed once you've found a scorpion in it, I think, but realize there's no point in saying it out loud.

One of Mom's bags is filled with last year's school papers. On top is my list of goals from Mr. Solomon's class.

→ *Fall in love*
→ *Figure out who the hell I am*
→ *Have sex without catching something*
→ *Repair my family*
→ *Escape*

I guess I could have done worse than four out of five.

Becky and I huddle around the speakerphone in Maurice's home office. Honey, call your friend, he's always telling me, Life is too short to worry about international phone rates. I try not to take advantage, but Becky comes over so we can talk to James when we can arrange a time.

Once Becky's recounted stories of her newspaper editorship ("Seriously, supervising sophomores is like the hardest thing ever.") and James has caught us up on London theater life ("If I have to hear about the rain in bloody Spain one more time…"), it's my turn.

So, Ms. Davis gave me the name of the talent rep at a new coffeehouse in the Village, I tell them, and I think I'm going to call.

Next to me, Becky squeals and grabs my arm. Why didn't you tell me? she asks.

He's telling you now, kitten. Lord, at least you'll be able to go watch and report back. But seriously, Michael. Do it. We need art to get us through this.

Because it's James, I call and sign up for a slot.

Then, there's one more call I make.

Connor said he heard Gay Men's Health Crisis was looking for volunteers.

I'm going to be stuffing envelopes twice a week after school.

It doesn't feel like a lot, but it's a start.

It's strange to have a spot in a showcase planned. An instrument to tune. Songs to write. Music to share.

And so I hop the D train, relish the smell of incense and pot in Washington Square, and find a spot near the arch, but not too close to where the break-dancers are working the crowd and passing the hat.

I lose myself in sound, the feel of my fingers on the strings, the light breeze. I close my eyes and let the world dissolve.

Until.

A feeling on the back of my neck, a racing of my heart that I barely remember.

I look up, and it's Gabriel's eyes that catch me. It was always his eyes.

My fingers stumble on the strings. I restart the measure. Stop. Force myself to laugh. Breathe. Hold myself back from running to Gabriel and throwing my arms around him.

I slow down. Bite my lip. Surrender. Pack away my guitar, my capos, my strap. Drawing out this moment of possibility.

My pulse betrays me by racing like that old wooden coaster at Coney Island, loud and out of control, surging forward at breakneck speed. I'm made of adrenaline.

I glance up, hesitant. Scared as hell. Filled with hope.

Gabriel is still there.

The other people drift away as I pack up. But he stands there, the smallest hint of a hopeful smile on his face.

He lifts his arms and goes into an easy cartwheel like the ones he did here for me before. Then he holds out his hands as if he's offering me a gift.

I shiver, wanting to reach out and touch him. Pull him into some dark corner and kiss until we run out of air.

I want to run my fingers over him, feel his skin under my hands.

I want to ask if he's found a way to go back to school and how his mother and sister are.

I want to tell him I've moved out and moved on.

I want to know that he's healthy.

Mostly, I want to tell him I still think about him all the time.

He steps toward me. I step toward him. He says my name just as I'm saying his, and suddenly, the world contracts so that our lips meet. Magnetic. Hungry. Holding on to everything we have. Everything that makes us human.

Time is a circle surrounded by a growing storm. And we're in the eye of it.

James says that things will get worse before they get better, and it's James so I believe him.

I don't know how I'm going to keep everyone I care about safe. Or if I can. Or what safe even means.

But I'm going to own my fear.

Own my voice.

Own my love.

Own my life.

And I'm not giving any of them up without a fight.

AFTERWORD

Ron Goldberg

The New York City of 1983—the world of *We Are Lost and Found*—was exciting, if dangerous around the edges. Stocks were high, rents were relatively cheap, and gay life was thriving, at least in certain neighborhoods. AIDS was a matter of concern, but not yet a crisis. In hindsight, I suppose we should have seen the darkening shadows, but at the time, it all seemed so unimaginable, and there was so much we didn't know about this newly named disease or how our city, country, and fellow citizens would respond to it. Or to us.

I was a twenty-four-year old gay man sharing a one-bedroom

apartment in Hell's Kitchen, several blocks north of where James and his roommates live. The neighborhood was dicey, its safety judged on a block-by-block basis. I lived on a "good" block, with a couple of upscale apartment buildings and restaurants. James—not so much.

I can't say for sure whether I saw the infamous article, "Rare Cancer Seen in 41 Homosexuals," when it was first published in the *New York Times* in July 1981—but I certainly heard about it. It was unusual enough for the *Times* to write anything about gay life—the paper refused to even use the term *gay* unless it was part of a quote or the name of an organization until 1987. But whatever concerns I may have had about this outbreak, it didn't translate into worry.

Besides, there was so much to enjoy about gay life in New York in the early eighties. There were fabulous gay dance clubs like The Saint, Twelve West, and the Paradise Garage. There were gay neighborhoods, like the West Village, where hot men cruised the streets in flannel, denim, and leather; the East Village, with its pierced punks and edgy artists, drag queens, and performance art; and the Upper West Side, where a strip of preppy gay restaurants and bars had turned Columbus Avenue into "the Swish Alps." And in the summer, you needed only to hop a ferry to be whisked away to the glamorous gay beaches of Fire Island.

Gay life had even begun to invade mainstream culture. There was the bisexual Steven Carrington on TV's top-rated *Dynasty* and gay-themed Hollywood movies like *Making Love*, *Personal Best*, and *Victor Victoria*. In 1983, Harvey Fierstein's *Torch Song Trilogy*—the play about gay life, love, and family that Michael sees with Becky—won the Tony Award, while the hottest ticket on Broadway that fall was the musical *La Cage Aux Folles*, about a "married" gay couple—the owner and the headline performer of an "exotic" drag nightclub—meeting their straight son's girlfriend and conservative family, complete with a cross-dressing chorus and the gay anthem, "I Am What I Am."

But this didn't mean it was safe to walk down the street holding your lover's hand.

Gay bashings were a regular occurrence, particularly in those neighborhoods we called our own. Often, it was just a bunch of teenagers "out for fun." Sometimes, they brought bats or metal pipes. Sometimes it was worse. Just two weeks before I moved into the city, a man with an Uzi shot up the crowd outside two gay bars in the West Village. The cops, who were largely unsympathetic, refused to keep statistics on anti-gay violence. Meanwhile, we couldn't even get the city council to pass a simple gay rights bill.

The truth was, whatever our gains in the fourteen years since the Stonewall riots, gay rights remained debatable, and gay lives expendable.

As if to prove the point, Ronald Reagan, who had been elected president in 1980, brought with him a collection of homophobic archconservatives and right-wing religious figures, who would come to embrace the epidemic as God's punishment for our "immoral" lifestyle.

But for the first few years of the AIDS crisis, politicians, like everyone else, simply ignored the disease and its victims. After a quick flurry of articles in the summer of 1981, there was barely any mention of this new "gay cancer" outside of the gay press. It would take nine months and more than three hundred new cases in twenty states before the *Times* published its next story, in May 1982, about the disease now called gay-related immune deficiency, or GRID. By the time the paper's fifth story appeared in August of that year, there were 550 cases, and the disease had a different name, AIDS (acquired immune deficiency syndrome), to avoid stigmatizing a caseload that now included IV-drug users, Haitians, and hemophiliacs.

The *Times* wouldn't publish another story about AIDS until January 1983, eight months later.

The lack of interest by the *Times* had a ripple effect—if a story wasn't covered in the "paper of record," it wasn't worth reporting elsewhere. As a result, there was *no* information available about this deadly new epidemic. We didn't have computers or smartphones. We couldn't google "AIDS" or look it up on Wikipedia. Instead, we were forced to rely on rumor and word of mouth and whatever was published every other week in the *New York Native*, our local gay newspaper.

But in 1983, there wasn't much to know.

We didn't know what AIDS was—how it worked, how you got it, or how it could be prevented—nor was it a priority for the Reagan administration to help us find out.

Looking back, you'd think it would have been a time of mass panic, but except for the occasional fear-mongering headline, AIDS remained largely under the radar. Unless you knew someone who was sick, the epidemic was something you were vaguely aware of, like background noise—a distant hum, not a siren. As far as we knew, it was happening primarily to a certain subset of gay men, mostly older than me, in their thirties and forties, whose fast-lane lifestyles included a lot of sex and drugs. And while I may have visited—and enjoyed—this world on occasion, I didn't consider myself a part of it. Nonetheless, I kept my ears open and eagerly read every issue of the *Native* as soon as it came out.

It was in the *Native* where, like James and Michael, I first read Larry Kramer's mind-blowing article, "1,112 and Counting," in March 1983. In it, Kramer describes a rapidly approaching holocaust, with nothing being done to stop it. Kramer is a central figure in the history of the AIDS crisis—a founder of both Gay Men's Health Crisis (GMHC), the first AIDS organization, and the legendary AIDS activist group ACT UP (AIDS Coalition to Unleash Power), and he is the author of countless angry articles and speeches, as well as the landmark play, *The Normal Heart.*

At the time, however, Kramer's feverish warnings were waved away by many in the community as the over-the-top ranting of a cranky, anti-sex hysteric. His article, while truly terrifying, was not at all empowering, and I saw little I could do beyond giving money to the cause and cutting back on my already limited number of sexual encounters. And since I didn't go to the baths or the back rooms and could name most of my sexual partners, I didn't really think I was at risk. AIDS hadn't invaded my circle of friends or pool of acquaintances.

Or so I thought.

Now it seems clear that many of my friends were, in fact, infected during this time and over the next few years.

Although initially controversial, the safe sex message in *How to Have Sex in an Epidemic: One Approach*, the pamphlet Michael finds in Connor's kitchen, would be embraced by a community desperate for some answers. Written by Michael Callen and Richard Berkowitz, two early AIDS activists who themselves were sick, their guidelines gave us our first real clue about protecting ourselves from this deadly plague. It wasn't the amount of sex you were having, they argued, but rather the exposure to body fluids, like semen and blood, that put you at risk.

But beyond the talk of condoms and the relative dangers of various sexual activities, their most revolutionary suggestion was that perhaps our best protection against this new disease might be love. That if we loved the people we were having sex with— even if it was only for a night or even an hour—we would not want to risk making them sick. It wasn't just about protecting ourselves, it was about protecting one another.

And so, like many others, I adjusted my sexual practices to safe sex only. And life went on.

Yes, I still had moments of panic, wondering if that bruise on my arm was the first sign of a KS lesion, or whether that sudden attack of diarrhea was the flu, food poisoning, or something worse. There was no "AIDS test," no identified virus or infectious agent, no idea of how long the disease might be incubating in your body. So, if you didn't die or wind up in the hospital with an AIDS-related infection, if you got better, you didn't have it and could assume that the Angel of Death had passed over your door.

And, yes, I was lucky. For many, AIDS was already a full-blown nightmare. People were dying terrible, horrible deaths in a matter of weeks, seemingly out of nowhere. They were subjected to abuse in city hospitals, ignored by attendants who were too scared to enter their rooms to bathe them or deliver their food. With no legal protection, people with AIDS—or even those suspected of having AIDS—could lose their jobs or be thrown out of their homes by terrified roommates, family members, or landlords. And when they died, funeral homes often refused to take their bodies.

The one bright spot was the response of the lesbian and gay community, including our doctors and health professionals, who banded together to create information networks and support organizations, providing care, companionship, and legal advice for people who often had nowhere else to turn.

It was 1983 when our community first began to show up in numbers, whether volunteering for newly formed AIDS organizations, participating in public vigils, or filling Madison Square Garden for a historic AIDS benefit. People with AIDS (PWAs) also stepped forward. Refusing to be defined by their disease and rejecting the label of victim, they drafted the Denver Principles, proclaiming their rights as people *living* with AIDS to have a voice in all research, treatment, and policy-making decisions about the disease affecting their lives. Their empowerment movement would soon spread across the country and later set an example for people with other diseases for years to come.

We wouldn't really begin to understand the full scope of the AIDS crisis for several more years, at least not until 1985, when HIV, the "AIDS virus," was identified and a test was developed. Even then, there was still more that was unknown than known.

But that's a story for later.

By the end of 1983, there would be more than 3,000

reported cases of AIDS and 1,283 deaths, with 42 percent of all cases reported in New York City.

So where does that leave Michael, James, Becky, Connor, and me? Living our lives. Looking for love. Calibrating the risks of both. Figuring out who and what is important to us, and how to become our best true selves.

And keeping a wary eye on the gathering storm.

Writer and activist **Ron Goldberg** *was a member of ACT UP (AIDS Coalition to Unleash Power) from 1987 to 1995, where he helped organize many of the group's most famous demonstrations, participated in countless zaps and actions, and served as ACT UP's unofficial "Chant Queen." Ron worked as research associate for filmmaker and journalist David France on his book* How to Survive a Plague *and enjoys speaking at high schools and colleges about the lessons and legacy of AIDS activism. Ron is currently working on a memoir about ACT UP and his life on the front lines of the AIDS crisis.*

AFTERWORD

Jeremiah Johnson and Jason Walker

Many things have changed in the nearly four decades since the first cases of AIDS were identified. In the early days of the epidemic, unnecessary fear was spread because people didn't know how the virus was passed on or that AIDS was even caused by a virus. That virus, HIV, is the human immunodeficiency virus, while AIDS is acquired immune deficiency syndrome, the condition someone can develop after years of having HIV. Without medicine, people living with HIV will typically develop AIDS in about four to eight years, at which time their immune system becomes unable to protect them, and they are at risk for multiple infections.

While we now know that only four types of bodily fluids can transmit HIV—semen, vaginal fluid, blood, and breast milk—in the 1980s, many individuals erroneously believed that HIV could be passed on through actions such as sharing a water glass, leading to even more stigma for affected communities. Thankfully, these days, we know that normal daily activities are not a concern; things like sharing utensils, toilet seats, hugging, and kissing are 100 percent safe.

In the early 1980s, there were a lot of major questions about this new virus and very few answers. It would take years of community advocacy and scientific research to turn that around. In 1983, no one was tested for HIV because no test existed until 1985. In the first years of the crisis, the only way to know if you had HIV was if you had already progressed to having AIDS and developed an AIDS-related illness. Now there are many options, including rapid tests using a drop of blood or saliva, which can provide results in twenty minutes or less.

There was also no treatment to prevent people from progressing to AIDS. It would take until 1996 for pills to be developed that could stop the virus. Early medication also caused serious side effects, and people living with HIV had to take several pills a day. Fortunately, today we have several options that are very well tolerated and require far fewer pills, in many cases just one per day.

We also know now that HIV treatment can help stop the virus from getting passed on through sex. This concept is called U = U, or undetectable = untransmittable. When someone on treatment gets the amount of HIV in their blood down to a point that we can't even measure it, then that person will not pass HIV on via sexual intercourse.

We've made significant progress in developing tools that help people stay HIV-negative. In New York, the epicenter of the U.S. HIV/AIDS epidemic, mother-to-child HIV transmissions have been essentially eliminated through standardized HIV testing and treatment as a key component of prenatal care. In the past, lack of access to unused syringes was a leading cause of increased HIV transmissions among individuals who injected drugs. The creation of syringe-exchange programs resulted in dramatic reductions in this population.

At the start of the epidemic, there was no guidance regarding sex; people in the affected communities were simply told to stop having sex indefinitely. Recognizing that that was not a reasonable solution, community members like Richard Berkowitz and Michael Callen (authors of *How to Have Sex in an Epidemic: One Approach*) developed guidelines for safe sex practices, including the use of condoms to avoid transmitting or acquiring HIV. But while condoms have unquestionably saved lives and prevented infections, they are not enough. Just like we see with contraception for women, human beings need choices. Fortunately, we now have other options.

In 2005, the Centers for Disease Control and Prevention (CDC) released guidelines for what we call *post-exposure prophylaxis*, or PEP (not to be confused with PrEP!). Taking the medication for twenty-eight days can significantly decrease the risk of getting HIV, though it must be taken immediately, and absolutely within seventy-two hours.

In 2012, the U.S. Food and Drug Administration (FDA)

approved Truvada, a once-a-day pill, for what we call *pre-exposure prophylaxis*, or PrEP (not to be confused with PEP!). By taking PrEP daily, someone who is HIV-negative can reduce their risk of getting HIV sexually by up to 99 percent. Many people compare it to oral contraception or the birth control pill for women. It can also reduce the risk for people who inject drugs by more than 70 percent.

While our understanding of the virus and the factors that lead to its spread has evolved—and less complicated and more tolerable HIV treatment and new prevention tools and strategies are available—these advances did not simply *happen*; they were victories won through fierce activism, which demanded justice and an aggressive government response to match the aggression of a virus likened to a plague. Many notable activist groups were formed including ACT UP (AIDS Coalition to Unleash Power), Gay Men's Health Crisis (GMHC), and Gay Men of African Descent (GMAD) to ensure that effective and safe drug treatment options were researched, produced, and made accessible to people living with the virus.

Faith leaders, nonprofit organizations, and politicians would later join the front lines of the AIDS movement and begin working on local and national levels to develop responses to an increasingly national and international public health crisis.

It is thanks to the bravery of these activists that we now have more tools and resources in our fight against HIV. And thanks to that progress, we are now able to have become even more aggressive in our fight to end this disease.

We have much more hope today. But not everything has changed.

We still do not have a cure. Treatment will keep someone living with HIV "undetectable," prevent the virus from being passed on, and allow someone to live a long, healthy life. But there are still many challenges to living with HIV, and treatment is not accessible everywhere in the world. A cure is still very much needed.

We still do not have a vaccine. PrEP is a great new option, but it's not always easy for everyone to obtain. If we want to reduce the nearly two million newly infected victims every year around the world, we need a vaccine.

And we still have enormous stigma.

What remains the same since 1983 is that HIV persists in communities that society and government marginalizes. Sex workers, drug users, people of trans experience, low-income communities, and people of color, particularly African Americans, are all disproportionately affected by this epidemic. Today, despite Black people being only 12 percent of the U.S. population, they account for more than 44 percent of new HIV diagnoses. Black people are more likely to die from AIDS-related complications than their white counterparts. While Latinx people in the United States account for about 18 percent of the population, they make up 26 percent of new diagnoses.

And worldwide, one million people died in 2017 from AIDS-related illnesses.

There is still much that needs to change; there are many fights that remain to be won.

We must advocate for research for even better tools to end HIV. We must continue to tear down barriers that keep people from accessing the tools we have now. As we start to see a resurgence of political and social climates similar to that of 1983—where proposed cuts to HIV funding loom and attacks on LGBTQIA communities and communities of color were commonplace—we are also seeing a resurgence of activism. We must retain the lessons of those who came before us and remain true to ourselves, hold on to that seed of hope that allows us to endure a pandemic that has claimed the lives of more than thirty-five million adults, children, parents, siblings, and loved ones globally, fight for the needs of communities most affected by HIV/AIDS, and, like Michael, always choose to love.

Jeremiah Johnson *is a New York–based HIV/AIDS activist focused on policy and research advocacy to end HIV as an epidemic in the United States and around the world. He has been living with the virus since 2008; following his diagnosis he obtained a masters in public health from Columbia University in order to better advocate for the needs of people living with and vulnerable to HIV infection. He currently serves as the HIV project director at Treatment Action Group in New York City.*

Jason Walker *joined VOCAL-NY as the organization's community organizer for HIV/AIDS campaigns in February 2013 after working for the Louisville City Council. His previous activism includes working with the U.S. Student Association and the NAACP, founding the first LGBT organization for people of color in Kentucky, and fellowships with the Center for Progressive Leadership, Young*

People for the American Way, and the Drum Major Institute.
He studied pan-African studies and cultural anthropology at the
University of Louisville.

ACKNOWLEDGMENTS

There are many people who left their marks on this book (and my heart) in one way or another, but two in particular deserve more gratitude than I could possibly put into words, although I'm going to take a stab at it, anyway.

Without question, writer and ACT UP activist Ron Goldberg is at the top of this list. We might have been thrown together by David France, but I echo Ron when he says it was *besherit* (divine providence). Ron is the truest *mench* I've ever met, and I'm grateful on a daily basis for his outstanding memory and ability to ferret out the most obscure bits of knowledge with great joy, his tough love, honesty, delightfully wicked sense of humor, and most of all his friendship (although his ability to talk me off ledges is a darn-close second). This book would have been a very different—and much lesser—thing without his input and guidance, and so would I. Thanks for helping me finish the hat.

My agent, Lauren MacLeod, has been a fierce and fearless source of support and brilliance. She's a rock star of epic proportions, and I don't know what I'd do without her. Her belief in this book when it was mostly smoke and mirrors constantly reminded me why I write. And I knew, when she told me to "throw in some more obscure '80s music" that she got it in all the right ways.

To the entire Sourcebooks crew: I know I tossed you a book filled with history, facts, politics, and lots of sensitive topics. And then I made it harder by writing this story in vignettes (!) with no quotation marks (!!). Thanks for loving it anyhow, and for joining me on this journey, particularly to my editor, Annie Berger; editorial assistant, Sarah Kasman; production editor, Cassie Gutman; copy editor, Christa Desir; and marketing guru, Beth Oleniczak; as well as cover artist Adams Carvalho.

Activists Jeremiah Johnson of Treatment Action Group and Jason Walker of VOCAL-NY gave generously of their time and knowledge to create their afterword to this book, and I couldn't be more appreciative.

Beth Hull and Shawn Barnes championed and strengthened this manuscript in infinite ways from the beginning, and I owe them both so much wine! Thank you for much-needed feedback, encouragement, and hand-holding to: Mia Siegert, Kate

Brauning, Rachel Lynn Solomon, Lisa Maxwell, Christopher Tower, Fiona McLaren, Suzanne Kamata (who I also owe for broadening my music tastes so many years ago), Carly Heath, and Carla Bartolomeo (thanks for sharing your name with Michael). Thanks also to the amazing musicians who made my 1980s so special, and to Zudfunck and John Patrick Shanley for unknowingly inspiring Becky's Dial-a-Daze recordings.

Special thanks to: Tom Wilinsky, my cloud's silver lining, who stepped in when I needed it most and offered me affirmations and thankfully distracting emails along with his friendship; Tami Davis, for answering odd religious questions in the middle of the night; Emilie Richmond, for being herself; Laurin Buchanan, for all those nights at The Bank and for collective mischief; and to Laura Richards, for having my back.

To Dr. Holly Hill, who taught me about theater, writing, and life (not necessarily in that order), I am always indebted. And, in a tragically belated note of appreciation, thank you to playwright William M. Hoffman, for taking time in 1985 to speak to a young drama critic with too many questions and probably not enough humility, about his (then) newly released AIDS play, *As Is*.

To my father, Harold Baker, whose devotion to staying informed in a pre-internet world resulted in him buying all of the New York newspapers on a daily basis, thank you for offering me a path to knowledge outside of our suburban town, for all the long talks, and for always being my biggest fan.

To John and Keira: If this book is about anything at its core, it's about love, bravery, and standing up for the things that matter most. Thank you for each demonstrating those in your own ways and for understanding how important this one is to me. I love you both more than hippopotamuses (but don't tell the hippopotamuses!).

Staying true to the facts and events of 1983's New York City was something to which I held myself highly accountable, so I have to confess to moving the release date of Frankie Goes to Hollywood's "Relax" up six months. Also, for those who go looking, while many of the settings in this book existed (and some exist still), The Echo isn't one of them. It's actually a mix of three clubs near to my heart (The Underground and The Bank in New York City, and Neo in Chicago, all of which have since closed).

Like Michael, Becky, and James, I came of age in the shadow of the storm that would become the AIDS crisis and later had the great privilege to work as a consultant for the AIDS Activities Office of a state government as a grant writer and program assistant. To those I worked alongside and met in that role and throughout the journey of writing this book, I can't thank you enough for sharing your stories and expertise. I hope I did it justice.

To Stuart, who keeps the flame of the AIDS Memorial's social media feeds lit, and to those who have posted their stories there, thank you for sharing your loved ones with the rest of us and for reminding us that #whatisrememberedlives. I urge every reader to follow this account and stand by my opinion that it's the most important thing on the internet.

Finally, to all who have worked and continue to work to eradicate this plague, to make the lives of those living with HIV and AIDS as long and equitable and as high quality as possible, and to those who educate younger generations, you are my heroes.

ABOUT THE AUTHOR

Helene Dunbar is the author of *We Are Lost and Found* and *Prelude for Lost Souls* (2020), as well as *Boomerang, These Gentle Wounds,* and *What Remains.* Over the years, she's worked as a drama critic, music journalist, grant writer, and marketing manager. She lives with her husband and daughter in Nashville, Tennessee. Visit her at helenedunbar.com, on Twitter @helene_dunbar, or on Instagram @helenedunbar.